Tales of the Were
Grizzly Cove

Bearliest Catch

BIANCA D'ARC

Copyright © 2016 Bianca D'Arc
All rights reserved.
ISBN: 1535087714
ISBN-13: 978-1535087711

DEDICATION

Special thanks to Peggy McChesney for her support and willingness to humor a crazy author. Thanks also to my family for giving me the opportunity to do what I love.

CHAPTER ONE

Drew had to be careful when he took his boat out now that Grizzly Cove was besieged by a creature known as the leviathan and its friends. From what everyone was saying, this leviathan wasn't from around here originally. Meaning, it wasn't from the mortal realm at all.

It was a creature from some darker, more magical place where evil ruled, and it had been let loose on the Earth's oceans by a bunch of unscrupulous assholes known as the *Venifucus*.

Drew knew a bit about the *Venifucus*. They were an ancient organization that had formed around the fey sorceress known as the Destroyer of Worlds. Her name was Elspeth, and she'd been banished to the farthest realms a few centuries ago after a series of major battles with the forces of Light that happened during the time the humans called the Dark Ages. They weren't far off with that moniker, since Elspeth was a major player among the forces of darkness.

Drew, himself, was an old soldier. He'd spent most of his life to this point fighting in all the hottest hellholes on Earth. He was also a shifter—a grizzly bear. So he was a bit more magical than most of his kind, but he'd only had to call on his innate magical abilities a few times in his life as a conventional soldier. Now that he'd retired with the rest of his unit and begun the social experiment that was the newly formed town of Grizzly Cove, Washington, he found himself using his magic more and more.

However, Drew's magical skills were a little bit different than most of his comrades. His talents lay in the areas of stealth. He had found out through trial and error that he could disguise his magical signature. He could erect a sort of shield, if you will, that would hide his magic—and that of anyone with him—from anybody who might be looking.

He couldn't cover large areas. He'd tried—without telling anyone else about his experiments—to shield the entire town once the attacks had started. Apparently, concentrating such a large group of usually-solitary bear shifters in one spot had made their little town an attractive target to the magic-sucking, soul-stealing leviathan.

But all his attempts to project his shield over a large geographical area had failed. He'd been able to shield his friends and comrades in small groups on foreign battlefields, but shielding the entire town was beyond him.

He had to have his shield up whenever he took his fishing boat out beyond the cove nowadays. He didn't want to become an appetizer for the leviathan or one of its smaller minions, but he still felt the call of the sea just as keenly as he ever had.

The peace and majesty of the ocean beckoned to him. Always had. That was one of the main reasons he'd jumped at the chance to settle in Grizzly Cove when his unit commander, John Marshall—who was also Alpha of this unlikely band of bears—came up with the idea to form a new community, camouflaged as an artists' colony, on the rugged Washington coast.

Settling on the coast sounded just about perfect to Drew, as was continuing to live near and work with the men he'd come to think of as his brothers during their years in Special Forces. They were family to him. Big John and the rest of the military bears were his people, and Drew would die for any one of them, as he knew they would for him.

Not that they had expected things to be dangerous in their new community. They were retired from active duty. Burned out. At least in his case. Most of the other guys hadn't been as close to the edge as Drew, but all of them were sick of fighting in mostly human conflicts all over the world. The luster of travel and being able to channel their beasts' natural aggression had played out, and it was time to settle down and find a mate—if they could.

Mates weren't thick on the ground for bear shifters. For one thing, there weren't as many female bears in any generation as there were males, so most males had to seek mates among other shifter groups or humans, if they were serious about not living out their long lives alone. John had put out a call for any bears who wanted to try life in Grizzly Cove to come join them. The town council—made up of the core group of the ex-military unit—vetted everyone.

They'd hoped to attract single female bear shifters, and a few had come to the area and moved in, which was a good start, but not nearly enough to meet demand. So the town council had begun to allow humans to open a few select businesses in town. The first, a bakery owned by three human sisters, had been a huge success. Not only did they make delicious breads and pastries, but the sisters were now mated to three of Drew's friends.

The second business the council approved had been a bit more problematic. Two sisters had opened a book shop, but what nobody had known when they applied was that the Ricoletti sisters were witches. Italian *strega*, they called themselves. It had all come right in the end, but the town council had decided to delay the approval of any more businesses or new residents until they could be sure they weren't letting more magic folk into what they had designed originally to be a bears-only town.

Plus, there was the leviathan problem. The elder of the Ricoletti sisters—Ursula—

had helped tremendously with that already. She'd cast permanent wards to protect the cove itself, though the leviathan and its smaller nightmarish friends were still waiting, just off the coast.

Ursula had mated the Alpha, surprisingly enough. Theirs was a true mating, it was obvious to see, and they were working hard to make the cove safe. Her younger sister, Amelia, was still unmated and reportedly working on some sort of potion-based magic that took a long time to prepare but would hopefully drive the leviathan and company even farther out to sea.

Meanwhile, Drew still took his boat far off shore, in defiance of everyone's advice. He knew he could hide his magic from the leviathan, and he also knew his inner bear needed the peace the ocean gave him. It was vital to his continued sanity. Drew needed the alone time and the quiet, with only the swishing of the waves against the hull of his boat and the soft sigh of the sea in his ears.

He fished, too, but it was mostly as an excuse to be out on the water all day. He supplied his buddy, Sig, with fish for his shop and made a little money off the bounty of the sea for his trouble. The other guys had all taken on different jobs necessary to the running of the town when they'd set up their community. Drew had created the job of fisherman and never looked back.

Oh, Sig fished too, but he stayed closer to shore, and he also ran a shop where he sold fresh fish, along with bait and tackle for those tourists who occasionally cruised through on their way down the coast.

All in all, Drew was happy with his new existence. He was slowly recovering from too many years as a soldier. The sea was his therapy, and it was working.

Drew popped open a beer after setting his lines and sat back in his favorite deck chair to enjoy the sunrise. He had a small piece of wood in his hands, and his pocketknife. Whittling occupied his mind in a good way, allowing him to relax a little, and the small figurines were fetching high prices in the art galleries in town, much to his surprise. He'd always liked carving miniatures, and if some silly tourist wanted to pay for his creations, so much the better.

He'd motored out while it was still dark, being careful to keep his magical shield up and running at all times. He didn't want to end up as a snack for the creature that haunted the depths out here, but he had to be out on the ocean when his internal demons came home to roost, as they had that night.

Bad dreams often drove him out, onto his boat, in the middle of the night. He was lucky that fishermen often set sail before dawn. None of his buddies really knew how tortured his sleep was. He'd been able to hide it from them so far. But alone on the ocean, he could forget his troubles and just...be.

Except...somebody was staring at him. Dammit. He'd felt this a few times before, but dismissed it. Now, of course, he thought he knew who it was.

A few days ago, a half-dead mermaid had washed up on shore, and his friend, Jack, who had taken on the role of game warden, had found her. He'd nursed her back to health, and the Goddess must have been at work, because they had discovered a mutual attraction that turned out to be another true mating.

The mer were some of the most mysterious of all shifters. Not much was known about them, but Jack's new mate—

her name was Grace—had been revealing little bits here and there. One of the things they'd told Drew in particular was that Grace's hunting party might be looking for her and that one mer in particular, a gal named Jetty, might have occasion to swim near his boat from time to time.

Grace had asked him to make contact with her friend, if at all possible, to let them know she was all right and staying on land for the time being, with her mate. Big John, the Alpha, had gone one farther and told Drew to deliver an even greater message. He'd offered the mer asylum in the cove while the leviathan prowled off shore.

That was a big step, and Drew knew it. Inviting another group of shifters into their territory was monumental and impressed upon everyone how dire the situation with the sea monster really was. Not that they didn't know already. Everyone had seen the thing attacking Ursula when she'd cast it out of the cove with her powerful, permanent, magical wards.

It had been like something out of a horror flick. Massive. Multi-tentacled. And so evil it reeked.

Drew was able to sense the creature and

its minions to some degree and was able to avoid areas where he believed they were lurking. Part of his magic, in addition to shielding, was sensing danger—and occasionally, he got a little tingle when he was being observed.

Like right now.

"Hey, mermaid, if you're the one called Jetty, I have a message for you," he called out.

He'd never tried to talk to her before. Of course, he hadn't really been sure what—or, in this case, who—was watching him before. He'd thought maybe it was a dolphin or something. He hadn't sensed any malevolence from the presence, just a sort of curiosity that didn't really set off his spidey sense for danger.

He figured now that he had some intel on what was watching him from the water, he'd try the direct approach. If that didn't work, maybe he'd dive in and swim around with the fishes for a bit. See if that got any response.

Though, of course, it was dangerous to go swimming with something that could breathe underwater when you couldn't. He'd be a little nuts to do it, but Drew liked to live dangerously. If he didn't, he'd have stayed safe in the cove, away from the sea monster and its evil children, and curious mer creatures who spied on him for no apparent reason.

He kind of hoped the mer would respond to his direct approach. He'd never seen Grace in her shifted form, and he was really curious about what mer looked like. In human form, Grace was just like any other person, though even Drew had to admit, she was a lovely woman. Jack had lucked out, finding such a beautiful and genuinely nice gal washed up on his beach. The Goddess had truly been smiling on the bastard.

"Your name *is* Jetty, right?" Drew tried again. "Grace told me you like to spy on my boat now and again. She's all right, by the way. She sends her regards. The leviathan cut her up pretty bad, but my friend Jack found her, and it turns out they're mates. You missed the ceremony, sorry to say."

"Grace is mated?"

The sultry female voice came to Drew from the port side of his boat. He got up from his chair and approached the rail, peering over slowly so as not to startle the mer woman.

Only her head and shoulders were visible above the water, but Drew had to clear his throat to buy himself some time. She was lovely in an otherworldly sort of way. Fine, pearlescent scales covered what he could see of her skin, making it flash in the sunrise, reflecting the peachy dawn light. Her eyes were the blue of the ocean and her hair slicked back and wet with ocean water. It was probably a deep black color, though he couldn't be sure it wasn't just a dark shade of brown. Either way, the combination of blue eyes, dark hair and pearly skin was breathtaking.

And her voice… He wondered if maybe she was a sea siren with a sound like that. He wanted her to talk more, but that meant he'd have to talk first. He cleared his throat again and tried to think of something sensible to say.

"Yes." There. That was simple enough, but she only smiled, waiting for him to say more. "Grace mated one of my friends. His name is Jack."

"So you said before," she replied, smiling in a way that told him she knew the effect she was having on him.

"Are you a siren?" he blurted out the

pressing question on his mind.

Her tinkling laugh sounded over the water. "No, lucky for you. If you ever met up with a real siren, your fishing days would be over."

He was transfixed by her voice anyway. And her laugh sent ripples of pleasure right through him.

"I don't know about that, Jetty. I can call you Jetty, can't I?" He tried for charming and was glad when it seemed to work.

"You may, but what is your name, sailor man?" Her tone was teasing, her voice challenging in an attractive way.

"I'm Drew. Short for Andrew. At your service." He wanted to touch her, but she was way down there and he was too far away. "Do you want to join me? I have a cooler full of beer and some ham sandwiches I'd be willing to share."

"Ham?" She looked skeptical. "Got any with cheese too?"

"As a matter of fact, I believe I do have a ham and cheese on rye along with the ham on wheat. The gals in the bakery set me up with a selection of sandwiches last night when I went in for dinner. I order ahead when I plan to spend the day out on the water."

"Do you have anything I can wear aboard?"

Sweet Mother of All, it sounded like she was going to accept his invitation. Drew scrambled, thinking fast about the articles of clothing he'd thrown onto the boat.

"I've got a terrycloth robe that would be large on you, but should serve the purpose. I've also got a change of clothes—a T-shirt and a pair of shorts—but they'd probably be too big for you. You're welcome to them, though." He was tempted to say she was welcome to anything he had, but that would be coming on a bit too strong for a first meeting. Wouldn't it?

"All right," she agreed, making her decision. "Get the robe and open the hatch on the stern. I'll jump up."

There was a utility door on the rear of the vessel that came in handy when pulling in overly large fish. He'd used it himself the very way she was proposing, so he knew it would work. All she had to do was launch herself out of the water and onto the boat. He used his grizzly strength to do it, but she was in her native element. Her tail would probably propel her upward, though she might land hard.

Drew frowned as he grabbed the robe from the inside the wheelhouse. He used it when he occasionally went for a dip, so he kept it handy. Moving to the stern, he tossed the robe onto a deck chair and opened the utility hatch, swinging the little door all the way open and out of the way. Then he stepped back and waited.

No way was he going to let her flop hard onto the unforgiving deck. He'd catch her in his arms and minimize the potential damage to her lovely, pearly skin.

The plan was half-formed in his mind when she burst through the surface of the water and jumped higher than even he could, aiming right for him. Her eyes widened as he held his arms out, reaching for her. Apparently, she hadn't been expecting him to be waiting.

But it was all happening too fast for her to change course. He plucked her out of the air, wrapping his hands around her waist and letting her fall against him. He slowed her momentum and took the brunt of her fall against his own body.

She seemed stunned for a moment after she'd come to an abrupt stop, held against his chest. He'd managed to keep them both upright, and his hands were still on her waist. He could feel for himself the slickness of her scales against his fingers and the rapid beat of her heart against his chest.

She was completely nude, but her scales covered her—just like his fur covered him when he was in his beast form. He was supporting her so her tail was kept from harm.

"You can put me down now, Andrew." Her voice washed over him, and he had to really reach to get his brain restarted. It had shorted out at the feel of her against him.

"Oh. Sorry." He lifted her in his arms and placed her gently on the deck chair. She had grabbed the robe before he deposited her and spent time wrapping it around her shoulders. He sensed her fussing with the robe was a way of hiding her embarrassment, and he tried to make it better. "I didn't want you to get hurt landing on the hard deck. You're okay, right?"

That shocked her eyes up to his. "I'm fine." She seemed to be looking for something in his gaze, but he didn't know what. "It was very thoughtful of you to catch me, but I jump up onto rocks much rougher than your smooth fiberglass deck all the time, so I would've been okay." She looked down again, busying herself with the robe, wrestling with it until she was covered completely.

Drew shrugged. "I didn't think of that," he allowed. Still, he knew he'd done the right thing. He couldn't have stood by while she flopped on the deck like a tuna. That wouldn't have been right. "Uh… Do you want privacy to shift? I can go into the wheelhouse, if you want."

Even as he asked the question he saw the scales recede from her face, replaced by pale human skin. He looked downward and realized her tail was gone. Two petite feet peeped out from under the hem of the robe now. She had already shifted to her human form.

"No need. As you can see, it's already done." She smiled at him, and even as he watched, her teeth went from pointy fish teeth to flat, human.

"That was fast," he commented. "Neat trick. My own shift is a lot more involved."

"You're a bear, right?"

He nodded. "Grizzly. Though my mother always claimed there was some mixed blood

17

back a ways. Either polar bear or tiger, she figured, since I love the water so much." And why was he telling her so much? Not even his teammates knew that bit about his ancestry.

"Sure it wasn't mer?" Her tone was teasing, but there was genuine interest in her eyes.

"Could've been," he allowed. "I haven't seen my mother in a while. Things have been…difficult…recently between her and me."

Jetty was quiet for a moment, then she reached out to touch the back of his hand. "I'm sorry."

The genuine concern in her voice floored him. They'd only just met, but he felt a connection with this mermaid like he'd never felt before.

He turned his hand over and clasped hers for a moment, squeezing lightly. "Thanks."

He hoped she understood the wealth of meaning in his words. He couldn't—shouldn't—speak of sensitive matters on first meeting a woman. He lived in hope that this first meeting with the mysterious mermaid wouldn't be the last.

She let go of his hand. She smiled, and

the mood lightened. "What about that sandwich you promised me?"

"Coming right up." He moved to the built-in cooler that was stowed under one of the side benches and lifted the lid.

Drew dug around in the ice chest for a few seconds, coming up with the big plastic bag that held the sandwiches in one hand, and two beers in the other. He lifted the beer toward her, an inquiring look on his face. She reached forward and took one of the bottles out of his hand, twisting off the cap and taking a sip while he sat down nearby and sorted through the bag.

"Ham and cheese on rye," he said, offering the wrapped sandwich with a flourish. She smiled, taking it from him. She opened it as he watched, working on his own sandwich more slowly.

It was clear she was eager to taste it. and she didn't waste any time taking a huge bite. The sensual groan that followed nearly made him hard. He watched her chew, her concentration fully on the sandwich, his own meal forgotten.

"Oh." She semi-groaned again, making him feel even warmer. "I'd almost forgotten how good land food tastes. This bread is fantastic. You said there was a bakery in town?"

He had to mentally slap himself to get his mind back on the conversation. She'd asked him about town. The bakery. That was it.

"Yeah, three human sisters run the bakery, and they're really talented with breads and pastries. They serve meals now, too. Just about everyone in town goes there a couple times a week. Even the recluses, like me." He had to smile at the stark truth in his casual words.

"Mmm. I can see why. This is delicious." She seemed to sober up a bit and looked over at him. "Thanks for sharing. I get a little tired of sushi after a few months."

He chuckled. "I bet." He busied himself unwrapping his own sandwich so he wouldn't blurt out something stupid, like a dinner invitation. *Too soon, Drew.* Way *too soon.*

"So tell me about Grace. I've been worried about her, and we've all been on the lookout, but it's rough times in the sea these days."

"Yeah." He frowned. "The leviathan gave us hell a while back, but a new member of our community managed to push it back, away from the actual cove. Before I forget, the Alpha wanted me to tell you that your people are welcome to take shelter in the cove, if you wish. Any creature who serves the Light is welcome during this crisis."

Jetty sat up straighter, her head tilting as if considering his words, surprise on her face.

"That's... More than I expected, actually. And mighty neighborly of him. I'll pass on the news to the others. I'm not sure if any of them will want to interact with you land dwellers though. Most of us are out here for a reason. And most of those reasons originated on land."

Drew held up one hand, palm outward. "That's okay. John was very clear that there were no strings attached to his invitation. The town council talked about this at length. We can't, in all good conscience, leave you out here to be slaughtered by the leviathan that was drawn here because of us."

"What do you mean?" She was intrigued, clearly, and the little furrow in her brow made him want to lean over and kiss it. *Down, boy.*

"The going theory is that by concentrating so many of our people in one spot, we unknowingly gathered a very tantalizing amount of magical energy here.

21

Which is probably why the leviathan and its friends came to call. It wants to feed on us. And on any other magical creature it finds in its path. You are in grave danger, and we're somewhat responsible, so we decided to grant safe harbor to those who wish it, now that the cove is protected."

"You're that sure of your protections? If we swam into the cove and it turned out not to be safe, we'd be trapped." Her tone was almost accusatory, but he understood.

"A lot has been going on in town. We allowed a few humans to settle among us. One of those turned out to be a powerful witch. Luckily, her special talent is to cast permanent wards. That's what she did around the cove. It's as safe as we can make it. And if, somehow, the protections did fail, you would have refuge on land, with us. We're not your enemy." Drew tried to sound both confident and friendly. "At times like this, all those who serve the Light need to stick together."

"Times like this?" She looked adorably confused. "You mean the monster you call the leviathan?"

"That, and the *Venifucus*. They're back in a big way, in case you didn't know. They've been targeting shifters and Others for years now, and actively trying to breach the barriers between this realm and the one where their leader is imprisoned. Some say, they might have already succeeded, though we're not sure about that. We only know it was probably a *Venifucus* cell that freed the leviathan and brought it back to this realm."

"Why in the world would anyone unleash that monster on us?" She sounded truly dismayed.

"To screw with us, mostly," Drew answered truthfully. "While we're preoccupied dealing with this situation, who knows what they're up to?"

"Bait and switch?" she asked, both intrigued and horrified if her expression was anything to go by.

Drew nodded. "You got that right."

CHAPTER TWO

The bear was incredibly good looking up close, just as Jetty had dreamed he'd be. But his words were giving her pause. He had lured her onto his little boat, but rather than the seduction scene she'd almost wished he'd carry out, he was giving her news that freaked her the freak out!

She had to stay calm, though. She was a rational being. She needed to tell her hunting party about this as soon as possible, but first, she had to know everything the handsome bear was willing to tell her.

The safe harbor offer was welcome news, and judging by his words and actions to this point, she felt she could trust him. The information about the *Venifucus* was appalling and downright scary. But she still needed to know exactly what had happened to Grace. The others would want to know.

"About Grace…" she prompted him, hoping he'd tell her what she wanted to know.

"She's good now, though it was a close thing. She encountered the leviathan and ended up beaching—which probably saved her life in the long run. She was hurt real bad, but Jack found her and patched her up. They mated soon after and are very happy. It was Grace who told me your name. Jetty, right?"

She realized she'd been rude. She still hadn't confirmed her identity, though he'd been very forthcoming with his information—and his lunch.

"Yes, sorry." She extended her hand for him to shake. "Jetty Silver. And you're Andrew…"

"Andrew Legine."

They shook hands, and damned if she didn't feel a spark of awareness sizzle right up her arm and into her heart. Was this it, then? Was the attraction mutual? She didn't really want to know for sure, because then, she'd feel obligated to act on it. Better not to know. Better to stay safe. At least for now.

She pulled her hand back.

"Um…why hasn't Grace been out to see us?" Surely, they weren't holding her prisoner?

Andrew chuckled. "They're newly mated."

"Yeah, so?" She didn't understand what he was getting at.

"They're still in their honeymoon phase. Probably will be for a while. From what I've observed, the urge to…uh…be together, among the newly mated, is something you don't ever want to mess with. Plus, Jack is super protective of her. He'd flip out if she went into the ocean by herself with the leviathan out there. And though I'm sure she doesn't want to admit it, I personally think her previous run-in with the creature was enough to scare her off. She almost died, Jetty. I don't think she wants to give that creature a second chance at her. Even after she'd recovered, she was still being lured by it." He let out a gusty sigh and ran one hand through his sexy long-ish hair. "Our shaman had to do some serious magic to break the creature's spell over her. It was a close thing, from all accounts."

"Really?" Jetty hadn't thought this through.

Newlyweds would want to stay close. The mating urge, it was said, was very strong. To the point where they wouldn't let each other out of sight for long. There were jokes among the mer about that sort of thing. Apparently, it was the same for other shifters.

And if a shaman had been called on to perform magic to break the creature's hold over Grace, Jetty could understand why her friend wouldn't want to chance another encounter in the open sea. She'd been lucky to escape with her life once. Going back would be tempting fate a bit too far.

"Grace told me to look for you. She told me your name and that you often saw me while I was out fishing."

Jetty felt a blush rushing toward her cheeks and decided a quick change of subject was in order.

"Why do you do it? Why do you still come out here when it's so dangerous?" She thought about it for a moment. "And why has the creature left you alone?" Suspicion reared its ugly head, but she didn't want to believe he was a bad guy.

He sighed heavily, dropping his head as if in defeat. "I can shield," he said softly, then raised his head to meet her gaze. "This isn't something everyone knows, so I'd appreciate it if you kept it to yourself." She nodded, and he went on. "I can shield my magic from detection, and I can sense what's around me. I know generally where the creatures are, and I go the other direction. I can avoid them for the most part, and shield myself so they don't find me."

"Can you shield others, too?" She'd heard of such magics, but they were rare, indeed.

He nodded. "If they're near enough, yes. Right now, you're under my shield, so you're as safe as I am. But if you swam away, at some point, you'll be out from under my protection and vulnerable again."

"Wow," she said, letting her feelings reign, sensing he needed to hear how impressed she was with what he'd just revealed. "That's pretty amazing." She got the impression he hadn't opened up about the extent of his abilities to anyone before, which made her feel special that he'd done so with her.

He shrugged off her praise. "Bears have a

lot of magic, generally. This is just something I can do that's a little different from my friends."

She thought it was probably a lot more than that, but she let it go. He was obviously uncomfortable talking about it, and she found she didn't want to distress him. She was actually coming to like the big bear shifter.

She had been intrigued by him from the first moment she saw him, dangling his fishing lines in the water from his little boat. He hadn't really seemed to care if he caught fish or not, and she had been perplexed enough by his behavior to stop and take a look. And a second look. And a third.

Before she knew what was happening, she was stalking the lazy fisherman, trying to figure out what made him tick. Why did he return to the sea, day after day, not really seeming to care if he caught fish or not?

He did catch a few, of course. More than a few, actually. He seemed to have the gift. The fattest fish continually sought to drown themselves on his hooks, and he took them aboard his boat, taking them back to town at the end of each day. Although, sometimes… Sometimes, he stayed out on the water for days. Living on his boat. Bathing in the sea in human and bear form.

The first time she'd seen him shift, her heart had raced. He was magnificent, both in bear form and in the human shape he had bared to take his beast visage. Tall, sleek and built for speed, he was well-muscled, in the way of Olympic swimmers. His hips were narrow, his butt firm, and his manly parts much *more* than adequate. She had blushed, even in her mer form, when she'd seen him naked for the first time…and every time since.

Truth be told, that was why she kept watching him. She'd been hoping to catch another glimpse of his perfect bod. And somehow…she just couldn't stay away. She had felt drawn to him for some reason. She didn't pretend to understand it, but she had been living on instinct ever since she entered the ocean, and so far, it hadn't steered her wrong yet. Some primal intuition pushed her to seek out the bear fisherman, and so she did.

And now this.

He'd just given her the most amazing news. Not only was the bear Alpha offering safe harbor to her people, but Grace—if

Andrew was to be believed—was happily mated. A true cause for celebration. There were so few mer in the vast ocean. It was a definite reason to party on those rare occasions when one found their true mate.

Jetty would have to verify all this independently, of course, but she thought she was a pretty good judge of character. He seemed on the level to her, and she suspected he hadn't said anything today that she'd discover later was false. Still, it was good to be cautious.

She'd long since finished her sandwich and the beer. Both had been a treat after all the months at sea. She missed the land sometimes, but she'd run to the sea to escape for a bit—as most of her people often did—and it had helped. She was almost ready to face land life again. But it would be on *her* terms this time. Nobody was going to dictate how she lived ever again.

She stood and loosened the tie on the robe, but didn't take it off. Since she was in her human form, she had a bit more modesty than when she wore her scales.

"I'd better go and tell the others what you've said." She walked toward the stern of the boat slowly.

"Is it safe to swim after a meal like that? I mean, most humans have to wait a bit before they go swimming after eating. How does that work for you?" He looked adorably confused and genuinely curious, so she humored his question.

"Once I shift, the mer characteristics win out, so it won't be a problem." She sent him a smile as she walked farther away.

It was hard to leave him, which surprised her, but she couldn't stay. She had responsibilities to her people, much as she would have loved to spend the rest of the day with the sexy bear shifter. He followed her, and they both stood at the stern of the boat, his hooks picking up nothing during their meal and continuing to just drift with no action.

"If you go a little northwest, you'll find some big sturgeon and halibut. The fishing is much better in that direction right now," she offered, hoping to help in some small way. "I might as well give you a solid tip on where to find dinner since you fed me part of your lunch." She turned to him, laughing lightly.

"The tip is appreciated, but you don't owe me anything, sweetheart."

The breath caught in her throat at his use

of the endearment. He also stepped right up to her, not a foot between their bodies as he looked down into her eyes. She almost forgot to breathe.

"But…" She didn't know what she was objecting to as his head drifted lower. Was he going to kiss her?

"Ssh," he soothed her, drawing her under his spell. "If you really want to repay me for the sandwich, all I ask of you is a single kiss."

What? Alarm bells sounded in her mind, but they were drowned out by the nearness of him. She could feel his warmth only inches away from her, and she wanted to snuggle up against him. She'd been so cold for so long…

Which was an odd thought for a mer to have. Mer didn't feel cold. The oceans were their home. So what had gotten into her now?

And why was she suddenly so eager to snuggle up to a land dweller? Oh, he was a shifter—they had that in common—but he still lived on land, and she in the sea. Though she could survive very well on dry land too. In fact, she'd spent most of her youth on land, with her family, doing the normal things that humans and shifters did. She'd gone to school, had friends, drove a car, had a job, and even moved in with her boyfriend.

But the situation with Dirk was what had driven her into the sea. She refused to go down that path again. Dirk had been human, a little voice inside reminded her. Andrew was a shifter. Maybe things would be different with a shifter.

Did she dare try to find out?

As his lips touched hers, all thoughts fled in the face of his passion. What started as a simple kiss turned into something much more profound within a single heartbeat.

He took her into his embrace, and she did get a chance to snuggle up to his warmth, basking in the feel of his strong arms around her. He kissed her lightly, at first, then gradually deepened the kiss when she made no move to push him away. His tongue danced with hers, showing her new patterns of pleasure even as her knees threatened to give way.

He was holding her up, his hands around her waist, supporting her, not imprisoning. And that was the key. He held her firmly, but lightly. She could break free any time she wanted...which was why she stayed.

How long she stood there, swaying with the swells that rocked the boat and rubbed their bodies together, she would never know, but it was Andrew who finally broke the kiss. When she would have gone back for more, he frowned at her, his eyes seeming almost as dazed as hers for a moment, before he seemed to regain his footing.

"It's coming this way. The leviathan. I feel it."

Dread washed over her, replacing all the warm emotions of moments before. "We have to run." She clung to his arms, fear making her voice shake.

He seemed to think for a moment, then nodded. "Do me a favor and reel in that line slowly. Don't jerk it. Don't draw any attention to us. Just move slow and steady."

He was already doing the same on the other side of the boat where another rod had swayed lazily in its holder. She moved to comply, trying to regain some sense of calm. His competent stance helped her focus. For just a second, she felt like, if Andrew was there with her, nothing bad could happen.

It was silly, she knew, but that was the impression he gave. He was so tall and strong. He seemed to know exactly what to do at all times and had a plan to lead them to safety, while all she could really do was panic.

But how did he know the creature was coming? That was something she couldn't sense out of the water. While she was in her mer form and in the ocean, she had instinct to guide her away from danger, but in her skin, on the surface, she was at a loss.

He'd said he could sense things. And shield things...

"Can't you shield the boat?" she asked in as quiet a voice as she could manage. She knew sound carried over the water, and she didn't want to attract any unwanted attention.

"I'm already doing it. But that only shields the magic. If we're here when it passes, it might still see us and decide to fuck with us just for fun. Who knows how this creature thinks? Or if it actually thinks at all," he muttered, stowing the rod, its line now fully spooled and out of the water.

Jetty followed suit with the fishing rod on her side of the boat. When it was stowed on deck, she tightened the loose knot on her robe. No way was she going back in the water until that monster had passed. Even she could feel the malevolence approaching now. The air was thick with a sense of doom that made her skin crawl.

She watched as Andrew started the engines and moved them swiftly away from the magical miasma that had been approaching their last position. He didn't speed, but he moved the boat with quick efficiency that earned her admiration.

"It won't follow the noise of the motor?" she asked, coming up beside him in the small wheelhouse.

"It might, but if it repeats the pattern of our previous encounters, it'll ignore us because of my shield. I think it's after magical targets, and right now, we don't look magical at all. Just another boat with uninteresting humans on it. Nothing to see here." He paid close attention to his instruments as he guided the boat away from the threat.

The heaviness in the air began to recede. She could feel the threat passing them by, off to the south.

"Almost there…" he said in a low, tense voice as he guided his boat away from the path of the creature with an expert hand.

Jetty couldn't feel it anymore, but Andrew

seemed to stay tense until a few minutes later, when he reached some point only he was aware of. They were within sight of the coast now, which suited her purposes well, though she wouldn't tell him that, because she didn't want him to know where her people were gathering...just in case.

"Did you feel that?" He was talking a little louder now, not quite as tense as he had been.

"Feel what?"

He cut the engine and let the boat drift. They were within sight of the shore, but not in danger of running aground any time soon.

"I told you about the permanent wards, right? We just passed into the outer reaches of the ward. The leviathan and its mini-me's avoid this area."

She was fascinated by the idea of a permanent ward, but she hadn't been able to feel anything specific. Then again, sensing such things was not her talent. She had good instincts, but that's as far as it went. Andrew, though... He seemed to really be able to sense things much more deeply than she would have imagined.

No wonder her people had gravitated to a nearby spot. It didn't just *seem* safer to their instincts—if Andrew was to be believed—it *was* safer. The bears of Grizzly Cove had done that. They'd made a small safe zone that extended out a short distance into the ocean. That went a long way toward convincing Jetty that the bears were honest in their offer of safe harbor. They seemed to care about the ocean beyond their land, which meant a lot to her.

Even before they knew about the mer colony that lived out here, they'd expelled the creature from their cove, but also did something to protect the shore and the waters just beyond. Sure, it made their settlement safer, but it also indicated a certain amount of concern for the deeps. Most land-dwellers never thought about sea life, unless they were fishermen or environmentalists of some kind. These bear shifters were like any other group, but they seemed to really care for Mother Earth—and all of Her bounty.

"One of our new residents cast the wards, but you should probably know that her sister is working on a better fix for the waters. She's been brewing potions of some kind for the past few weeks, and when she's ready, she's going to attempt to purify the waters and make it so that only creatures of good intent can approach the cove from the ocean."

Jetty wasn't sure what to make of that.

"Do you intend to make it impossible for anyone to swim into the cove without your knowledge?" If so, that was a pretty rotten deal for the sea dwellers.

"No. From what I understand, it doesn't work like that. The magic she intends to cast will be to keep evil out. Like I said, as long as the intentions are good and the person or creature isn't a servant of evil, they'll be welcome in the cove. I don't think any of us have any interest in monitoring every single creature in the ocean on their way into and out of the cove. Nobody's got time for that. We all have a wild side, and we know what it means to be able to roam free."

She heard the truth ringing in his words, but she was still skeptical.

"But what if your Alpha or town council decides otherwise?" she challenged, just to see what he'd say.

"Honey, I'm on the town council. And our Alpha rules at our pleasure. Bears aren't like other shifters in that we follow the Alpha blindly. We *chose* John to be Alpha because he's our best strategist, but we don't do every little thing he says merely because he has the title. Bears are independent thinkers. The core group that makes up the town council is all ex-military too. We were all members of the same Spec Ops unit, and John was our commanding officer. We've spent a lot of years working together, and we're like brothers. I know them like I know myself, and none of us have any interest in shutting off sea access to the cove. We're more concerned about building a life here and finding mates. We just want to live in peace and be happy."

His words ran true in her ears, and she realized the bears weren't that much different from her people.

"Isn't that what everybody wants? To live free and be happy. It's a worthy goal." Her tone was contemplative as she looked out over the water.

He'd given her a lot to think about, and she definitely needed to go back to her people and tell them all the news. Things were changing rapidly, and there were decisions to be made.

"Well. I guess this is my stop." She untied the robe again and let it fall to the deck at her feet before diving swiftly off the boat.

"Wait!"

She heard him call out even as she hit the water. If she'd given him time to talk her into staying, she never would have left. Better to do it fast. Make a clean break. The bear-man was just too enticing.

She felt her change come over her, legs fusing into a tail, scales rippling over her skin. She worked her way to the surface again, just to get one last look at him, unable to help herself.

He was leaning over the rail, a look of dismay on his handsome face. His expression changed to relief when he caught sight of her again, which warmed her heart.

"Will I see you again?" he asked, warming her further.

She smiled, knowing he'd see the sharper teeth, the alien side of her being that she seldom put on display to outsiders. Sure, he was a shifter too. He had a beast half. But his beast was something humans were used to seeing. In her case, she was something mythological—and the mer had worked hard over the eons to keep it that way.

"I believe our paths will cross again, Andrew," she told him, her words only slightly affected by the changes in her mouth brought on by the shift.

"How will I find you?" he wanted to know.

She couldn't tell him. It was one of the most important rules of being mer. Mystery was their friend. It kept them safe. She could never reveal the secrets about where the mer lived or how to find them. Not to anyone.

"I'll find you, my new friend. Your boat isn't hard to spot."

As she swam away beneath the waves, she couldn't get him out of her mind. They would meet again, but she had a lot of things to do first. Briefing the others was the first task. Then, she'd have to do a little reconnaissance of her own. If all went well, she'd be seeking out the handsome bear shifter sooner than he might think.

Even her cold fish side warmed to the idea of getting close to him again. He kissed like a dream, and she had been unable to find any fault with his words or manner. If everything he'd told her checked out the way she thought it would, she would feel free to let loose a little more with him. It had been far too long since she'd been with a man, and she'd never been with a shifter.

She wondered what it would be like to be with someone from whom she didn't have to constantly hide her dual nature. Would it be as freeing an experience as she thought? Or would such a relationship carry its own unique problems?

There really was only one way to find out. The next time she saw him, she was going to do all she could to seduce the man and see where it led. If she'd been a land dweller, she would have growled at the thought of getting him naked and seeing if his performance lived up to the potential advertised by his good looks.

If she'd been a shier creature, she would have blushed at her own thoughts, but Jetty was known for being one of the bolder of her people. She'd put that bold nature to good use the very next time she saw her bear, and she vowed, he wouldn't know what hit him.

CHAPTER THREE

Jetty swam into the cove, enjoying the splendor of the place. It really was a nice little inlet, protected from the ferocity of the ocean. The waters were calm, and even though the sky was overcast, as it often was in this part of the world, enough light filtered through to make the vista below the surface a lovely blue-green teeming with life and beauty.

She was a woman on a mission. She intended to spy on the land dwellers of Grizzly Cove to see if she could determine how truthful Andrew had been with her the day before. Telling the rest of her hunting party everything he'd told her about the ongoing battle with the evil creature in the sea that they'd all been hiding from for the past several weeks didn't take long. Opinions were mixed on whether or not they could trust the bear shifters and their offer of safe harbor. Which was why Jetty had volunteered to swim into the cove and see what she could discover.

She had been told to use her best judgment on whether or not to make further contact with the bear fisherman. Since she was a proven scout, the elders left the decision up to her. Jetty was honored by their trust in her abilities, which made it all the more important to get this right.

She spent the entire day spying on the various residents on land, as best she could. She had better luck when she hid beneath the pier behind the small bait shop and listened in on the conversations between the proprietor and his customers. They were all shifters, as far she could tell, and they spoke freely among themselves about many topics.

The most interesting to her, of course, were the few mentions made about the new permanent wards and how much safer it was in the cove since they had been cast. Jetty discovered that the witch who had done the work was now mated to the Alpha bear. Andrew hadn't told her that—probably wanting to keep the identity of such a powerful witch secret until he was sure of Jetty and her people.

She didn't begrudge him that. They all had secrets to keep and judgments to make. And they both had responsibilities to their people, to keep them all safe.

From the way the shifters talked, it was clear the Alpha's new mate had earned their respect. Jetty knew that shifters and magic folk rarely worked together in this day and age. That they had welcomed a witch into their town said something about this group's tolerance and willingness to work together to defeat evil.

If they had forged an alliance with two powerful witches, then maybe they were serious about wanting to offer safe haven to the mer. And perhaps, the mer could work with these shifters to help fix the big problem in the ocean—what they had named the leviathan.

Jetty had kept an eye out all day for signs of Grace, but her friend hadn't come near the water. If she really was newly mated, Jetty supposed Grace was probably spending a lot of time with her mate, on land…most likely in a bed. Jetty almost envied her old friend. Grace deserved a little joy in her life, and if she really had found her mate, Jetty was happy for her.

The jury was still out, though. Jetty would have to see Grace first, to believe it. So far, she'd been able to confirm a lot of what Andrew had told her. The town seemed exactly as he had said it was, and she was almost ready to take her reconnaissance to the next level. But first, she had to find Andrew's boat.

Drew couldn't sleep. Again. So what else was new?

He levered himself out of bed, knowing this would be one of those days he spent out on the water, away from everyone, seeking solace in the peace of the ocean. He didn't know why, but the water soothed him, even when the weather wasn't ideal. Which looked to be the case today. He could smell fog in the air and moisture that meant rain later. Great.

But it wouldn't deter him from going out. On days—scratch that—nights like these, he had to get out on the water.

He dressed haphazardly, grabbing a bag filled with sandwiches out of the fridge on his way out the door. The gals at the bakery kept him stocked. When he stopped in there each night, he walked out with a bag of sandwiches for the next day. It was just easier that way.

Drew headed out the back door of his house. It was a small place, close to the water. The best feature of the land he'd chosen to purchase and build on was the dock. He had built it himself, and it was in a part of the cove deep enough that he could easily keep his boat there, ready and waiting for him whenever he wanted to go out. The setup was ideal.

Fog wisped around his ankles as he walked out onto the dock. He was about to toss his stuff onto the deck when he realized he wasn't alone.

"Hey, sailor, come here often?"

A mermaid was sitting in the mist at the end of the dock. Not just any mermaid. Jetty. Lovely Jetty with the dark hair and pretty eyes.

"Often enough." He changed direction, walking the length of his boat, out to the end of the dock. When she didn't move, he sat down beside her, his toes dipping into the water below. "I'm glad to see you again. To what do I owe the pleasure of this visit?"

"I told you I'd find you." Her tone was flirtatious, her scales glimmering faintly in the misty fog. It was still dark out. An hour or more left until dawn. "I've been checking out what you told me the other day, and I'm cautiously optimistic that we can take it to the next level."

Whoa, momma. What, exactly, was she talking about? Did she mean…?

He wasn't sure what she meant, but his mind went immediately to the sex place. How could it not when he'd relived that kiss over and over since it had happened?

Maybe he ought to slow down a bit and find out what she meant before he went off half-cocked. And there he went, to the sex place again.

"Next level?" he asked, barely able to form those two words. She smiled at him as if she knew exactly what was going through his mind.

Little minx. She probably did. He found himself torn between frustration and admiration. He liked that she was comfortable enough with him now to tease him.

"The part where I come ashore and you show me around, maybe introduce me to some of your friends. Of course, I'll want to see Grace first, if possible. And depending how that goes, I'd like to talk to your Alpha, if he has time for me." She smiled at him in the darkness, and he was enchanted. This woman had a magic all her own. "The thing is, I don't have any clothes here. Would you be willing to find something for me to wear?"

She wanted to see the town. Well. That was progress. Suddenly, his plans for the day took an unexpected turn. He'd postpone the boat excursion. Ushering Jetty around town was a much better prospect. There was something about her that just... He just liked being near her. He wouldn't examine it much closer than that right now.

"I believe I can arrange something. I have some things that might fit, but if you want more...uh...feminine stuff, we could ask Grace. Jack mentioned that she'd had her stuff shipped up here." A thought occurred to him. "I can see now that, if we're going to host your people in the cove, we should probably make some allowances for this kind of thing. We can talk about it with Big John, the Alpha. I'm sure he'll make time to meet you, and he's great at strategy and logistics."

"Sounds good," she agreed, her scales sparkling faintly. "Now, if you'll just get me something to put on, I'll shift, and we can move this discussion to dry land."

Not wanting to go back to the house, lest she somehow change her mind and swim away, Drew jogged over to his boat and jumped aboard. His robe was still where he'd left it, and when he hopped back onto the dock, Jetty was already standing on the end, on two luscious legs. She had her back to him, her skin glistening with water in the dark before dawn. He walked up to her slowly, admiring the sight she made standing there, on his dock. He held the robe open and came up behind her, wrapping her in it. She put her arms into the big sleeves and tied the belt around her trim waist, smiling up at him over her shoulder.

He wanted to kiss her right then and there, but she began walking up the dock, her feet finding a natural rhythm with the slowly moving wood under them. He watched from only a few steps behind her as she approached the spot where the floating dock met the shore, and he saw her hesitation.

"Is everything okay?" he asked quietly, not wanting to spook her.

"I haven't been on land in years," she replied, pausing before taking that final step.

She said nothing further as she made the transition from the floating wooden platform to the beach. When she tried to walk, she faltered a bit, but Drew was there to steady her, putting one arm around her waist and taking one of her hands in his as he came up beside her.

"Lean on me, if you have to," he told her. "Until you get your land legs." He chuckled, and she followed suit.

"Crazy, huh?" she asked rhetorically as they moved slowly up the beach toward the house. "I get so used to the motion of the ocean after a while that it's disorienting to be on solid ground that doesn't move."

"Oh, it moves occasionally. We had a small tremor just the other day, in fact," he corrected her with humor. "But generally speaking, earthquakes are a bad thing. They make my bear side want to run."

"Smart bear," she observed, steadily gaining her footing as they went along. "So where are you taking me? Is that your house?"

"Home sweet shack," he confirmed in a self-deprecating way as he ushered her along the path he'd put in that connected the beach to his back door.

She paused, looking up at the two-story structure. "This isn't a shack, Drew. It's lovely." Her admiration of his handiwork made him feel warm all over. "The view from upstairs must be phenomenal."

"Yeah. That's my bedroom window," he told her. "You're welcome to check it out. Anytime."

He couldn't help himself. His voice dropped to a low rumble, thinking about her in his bedroom. Oh, yeah. He wanted her there. In his bed.

If she wasn't much mistaken, the werebear had just issued a naughty invitation in that growly voice of his. Jetty had to suppress a shiver of delight just hearing him speak in those low, sexy tones.

He opened the door for her, and she walked into an unexpected delight. The house was like something out of a designer's showcase. It had a nautical feel. Everything was light and airy. White dominated, but polished wood and brass accents were thrown in here and there, adding to the appeal of the place.

"This is really gorgeous." She couldn't keep from voicing her approval. The place was perfect. And clean, which she hadn't expected of what she assumed was a bachelor pad. The thought made her stop just inside the door. "You're not mated, are you?"

He actually laughed. Just one short bark of disbelieving laughter as he closed the door behind them and walked past her, into his home.

"No. I'm not mated. Why do you ask?"

He led the way farther into the house, and she followed, impressed with each new revelation. The kitchen at the back of the house was immaculate and state of the art. There was a small dining room, and the front room was decorated in leather and wood. Very manly, yet elegant and inviting.

"It's just…so clean. And gorgeous."

"And men are slobs, is that it?" He paused to look back at her, a sparkle of humor in his deep brown eyes.

"Well, I didn't mean to insult your entire

gender, but the men I've known haven't exactly been neatnicks." Her gaze swept the room, taking in the beautiful furniture, comfortable design and personal touches here and there that told her this was his space. "My ex was a disaster. If I wasn't there to pick up after him, his apartment would've been condemned."

Did he just growl? She couldn't be sure. It was almost a sub-vocal sound, but she could've sworn…

"I'll go up and get some clothing that might fit. Unless you want to come up and get the full tour. There's a bathroom up there if you want to change in there."

Something inside dared her to go upstairs and see more of the bear's private domain. She liked being with Andrew, which was odd because it had taken her a lot of time to work up to moving in with her ex-boyfriend—Dirk the Jerk. As a mer, she was more than a bit of a loner, but she'd wanted to see if she could find a mate on land. Unfortunately, she'd picked the wrong man. Oh, *boy*, had she picked the wrong man.

"I'll come up," she said softly, following where he led. Andrew stepped back to allow her to precede him up the stairs, and she wondered if he was trying to check out her ass under the bulky terrycloth robe.

His bedroom was just as lovely as the rest of the house. Done up in blues and greens that reminded her of her ocean home, she could easily picture herself luxuriating in this private oasis. If she had a house, she'd decorate her own place in much the same style.

Andrew had gone straight to the dresser and started opening drawers. He grabbed some things and turned toward her, holding up a dark blue T-shirt that was probably snug on his massive physique, but that might possibly not look too baggy on her much smaller frame.

"How about this?" He waited for her to nod before handing over the shirt. Then, he held up a pair of board shorts that had a string at the waist. "And these? They'll be a little big, but you can pull up the slack on the string."

She held out her hand again for the shorts. "They'll do. Beggars can't be choosers, and all that. Actually, this is better than I'd hoped for, but maybe we could make Grace our first stop? She might be able to help me not look like a bag lady if we go into town later." She chuckled at her own observation and was glad when he followed suit, not taking offense.

"It's a bit early. How about I make you some breakfast here, and then, we'll give Jack and Grace a call to see if they're ready for some company?"

It sounded a reasonable plan to her, and she told him so. He pointed her toward the bathroom, which was attached to his bedroom, or gave her the option of just closing the door to his bedroom, promising not to intrude. In fact, he headed for the stairs, telling her he was going to start working on breakfast while she changed.

That left her alone in his private space, and she couldn't help snooping just a bit after she hopped in his giant shower for a quick rinse before putting on the fresh clothing. Once in human form, she didn't necessarily like the feel of the salty ocean residue on her skin. It chafed. So the shower was a necessity.

The clothes weren't too bad of a fit, but her nipples insisted on poking little points against the soft fabric of the T-shirt. He'd notice. And there wasn't a blessed thing she could do to hide it without a bra. She'd hunch over as much as possible and try to keep the baggy garment from showing him just how much she liked his scent until she could get some decent under things.

But holy seaweed, she liked the way the werebear smelled. His T-shirt was freshly laundered, but under the faint odor of the unscented detergent he favored, his scent still clung to the porous fabric. It was subtle, but it was there, and she reveled in wearing it next to her skin. Her inner beast got feisty when it smelled him. It wanted to swim with him. It wanted to lure him closer. It wanted to mate with him. *Bad.*

Her human side figured it would be so, so *good.*

Hold your seahorses, Jetty. She had to finish her mission here, on behalf of her people, before she could entertain all those carnal thoughts inspired by the hunky fisherbear.

The scent of bacon wafted up the staircase as she looked around his room unashamedly. He had a few personal mementoes decorating his space. A few photographs had been blown up and framed to hang on his walls, the most prominent of which was a group shot of a bunch of muscular men in soldier clothes. Ooh-la-la, there wasn't a clunker among them, but the most handsome, by far, was tall, lean, brown-eyed, chestnut-haired Andrew.

He'd been a soldier. And she'd bet most of the men in this photo were also shifters, and probably residents of this town. It was time to find Grace, and then, if all was well, go out and meet some more of these werebears. Her people were leaving it up to her judgment as to whether or not they'd accept the safe harbor offered by the Alpha.

She'd have to meet with him too, once she'd seen Grace and a bit more of the town. She would have to get a feel for the man and whether or not he could be trusted. Grace's opinion would go a long way toward helping her decide as well, but Andrew was right—it was too early to bother Grace and her new mate. They'd have to wait until dawn, at least.

In the meantime, she was going to enjoy eating cooked food for the first time in a long time. She'd really missed bacon.

Following her nose down the stairs and back to the kitchen, she found Andrew wielding a spatula in front of his gourmet stove. He looked comfortable cooking, and he had the tightest ass she'd seen in a long,

long time. She stood in the archway that led into the kitchen, just watching him for a moment.

He really did have a world-class ass. Certainly a lot better than Dirk the Jerk's. They weren't even in the same universe. Dirk had been an actor. He was good looking, but human. He'd kept himself in shape, working out with his personal trainer every day, but his sculpted looks were designed to please. Andrew was a man at his peak—designed by Mother Nature, as the Goddess intended.

In his case, the Goddess had outdone Herself.

Drew fried eggs and made toast. He wasn't sure what she might like, so he made a little bit of everything. His inner bear wanted to feed her. To take care of her.

When he turned around and found her watching him, he smiled at the look on her face. If he wasn't much mistaken, he'd caught her ogling him.

"What do you think?" he challenged, a big of deviltry running through him.

"About what? The food?" She took a cautious step into the kitchen, seeming unsure. He liked throwing her just a little off balance. She seemed like the kind of woman who enjoyed repartee, which was good because he liked it too.

"No. About my ass. You were just checking it out, weren't you?" He slid two plates full of food onto the kitchen table as she paused her steps, her mouth dropping open.

"Was not," came her immediate denial.

"Were too." He winked at her, grinning broadly as he finished bringing things to the table.

He liked teasing her. She fumbled a bit with embarrassment, but then, he saw the moment when she decided to give as good as she got.

"In a purely aesthetic way, it's not bad." She tilted her head to the side, looking him up and down.

"What? The breakfast?" He played along, wanting to prolong the banter.

"No. Your ass." She giggled, breaking the serious pose in the most adorable way.

He wanted so much to take her in his arms and kiss her senseless right at that very moment, but it was too soon. She'd only just come to him. They hadn't had time to build trust. She hadn't had time to get to know him and discover what kind of man he was...or that he'd sooner die than hurt her in any way.

Whoa.

He shook his head at his own thoughts. It was too soon to be thinking that way. Wasn't it?

He waited for her to be seated before taking his own place at the table. His mama would tan his hide even today if he didn't act like a gentleman when there was a lady in his presence. And his mama was not a woman to be trifled with.

Jetty smiled at him and bowed her head for a moment. "With thanks to the Goddess," she said briefly, surprising him by praying before she picked up her fork.

He let the moment stretch while she began to eat, and he followed suit. The quiet of the earliest part of the morning surrounded the house and permeated through the walls into his kitchen. It was usually a lonely time of day for him, when he was running out to his boat, his demons chasing him from sleep and sending him to the water.

But today, all that was different. He had

Jetty in his house now, and it was as if her presence had chased the demons away altogether. As if they couldn't stand in her presence.

Wasn't that a wonder?

"Are your people generally religious?" he asked, trying to make quiet conversation.

"We usually thank the Goddess before we eat, but that might just be my pod. I don't know about other groups. In water, the thanks are silent, but when on land, we can do it either way—silent or spoken."

"It's important to you," he observed, eating his toast.

She shrugged. "It's habit and shows respect for the lives of the fish we hunt so that we may continue to live. So, yeah, I guess it is important to me. But it isn't to you?" She looked at him, frowning a little.

"On the contrary. My mom always had us give thanks before every meal. Of course, she's a priestess, so..." He let the sentence drift off as he concentrated on his meal.

He could feel Jetty's surprise, but he didn't look up. He had no idea why he'd just revealed that about his mother. Even his teammates hadn't learned about his mother until after he'd been injured so badly he had to be sent back home. Only then had Big John become aware of Drew's circumstances. Mom had met his stretcher at the airport and taken charge from there.

His teammates had been duly impressed with her resources and intensity. She wouldn't let him die, and he knew he could thank her for the fact that he'd survived. Now he just had to get his head screwed on straight again before he could face her, but he knew she understood.

His mother had been the one to advise him to go to Washington and rejoin his friends. She'd said it would be good for him, and she hadn't been wrong. Drew was doing a lot better since rejoining his unit and working with them to fulfill another mission—this one the oddest of them all, but the most valuable long-term. They were building this town from the ground up, and it felt good to be part of the team again.

"Your mother doesn't live close?" she asked softly after the silence had stretched a bit.

"No. Though she and dad are thinking about moving here eventually, but I told them not to come just yet. Not until we've made it safer. I couldn't tell her why or she'd have been here like a shot, trying to help. I just don't want her in so much danger. She's supposed to be slowing down, teaching the next generation, but her most recent apprentice is almost done with her studies, and Mom will probably be nosing around here sooner than I want. She's really curious about this experiment."

And why in the world was he being such a Chatty Cathy today? Drew put it up to Jetty's influence. Something about her made him want to open up and tell her his life's story, which totally dismayed him. What the hell?

"My folks live in Los Angeles," she offered. "I lived there, too, until a few years back when I dove into the ocean and decided to stay for a while."

"After you broke up with your ex, by any chance?" He pried a little, wanting to know more about the ex that she'd mentioned before. His jealous bear wanted to claw the dude and make him bleed.

"How'd you guess?" She made a face and forked up more eggs, stabbing them like she was stabbing her ex.

"Sorry. I didn't mean to bring up bad memories." He tried to convey comfort in his softly spoken words.

"No. It's okay. I was dating an actor, and I thought it was serious. I didn't realize he was just playing the role of besotted boyfriend to get what he wanted. Eventually, I moved in with him, giving up my apartment and most of my stuff because his place was small and we couldn't fit it all. I put many of my things in my parents' garage, thankfully. But when the breakup happened, it was sudden, and I only stuck around long enough to pack up my things, drop them at my parents' and take off for the water. I've been living in the ocean ever since. Things are a lot simpler there."

Drew nodded. "I bet. And I'm sorry you had a bad breakup, but I'm glad you kicked the jerk to the curb. I could go kill him for you, if you like."

CHAPTER FOUR

Was he serious? He looked awfully serious.

"No, it's okay," she was quick to say. She didn't want him killing anyone and going to jail for her. "I put it behind me, but it's funny you called him a jerk. That's my little name for him. Dirk the Jerk."

"His name is Dirk?" Andrew's expression was far too calculating for her comfort.

"Yeah, but it's really okay. I don't want him dead." *At least not anymore.* "And I do my own killing, these days." She chuckled. "I'm part of a hunting party that fights predators near the pod to keep the rest safe."

"You're a warrior." He seemed surprised by her revelation.

"Didn't Grace tell you?"

"No. She's only shared a little with her mate, but he's kept quiet. They must've told John the few things he needed to know to trust her. We all understand about needing to protect our people's secrets, and we generally respect each others' privacy."

She thought about that for a moment. "Things are easier in the ocean. We don't have to dodge humans and their laws much. Living on land, surrounded by them, and the possible threat of them, is hard."

"But you lived on land for a while, right? You lived with your folks and your ex," he prompted.

She sighed. "Yeah. I grew up on land. I didn't flee to the ocean until after…"

"After you broke up with Dirk the Jerk," he supplied, finishing her sad thought.

"I totally ran away from my troubles," she admitted. "It was cowardly, but the ocean has a way of washing away all your troubles, you know?"

She looked up at him, hoping he'd understand, and she saw more than she bargained for in his eyes. He nodded slowly.

"I know. Why do you think I'm always out on my boat? I crave the peace of the water, but you must know the ocean in ways I could never experience. I envy you, in a way."

She hadn't expected that.

"What are you trying to forget?"

She saw him withdraw at her direct question, sitting back in his chair and looking down at his empty plate. She'd pushed him too far, too fast. For a moment, she considered reaching out to him. Apologizing. But he stood from the table before she could make a move toward him and headed for the sink with his empty plate.

"It's complicated," he allowed, at least giving her the courtesy of some kind of answer as he rinsed his plate and then tucked it into the dishwasher rack. "A sad story for another time. Right now, I think it's time to call Jack and Grace and see if they're ready to come up for a little air so you can see your friend."

He pulled a slim phone from his hip and hit a few buttons, then held the device up to his ear. She could hear it ringing, and then, a deep, male voice answered. The earpiece was set loud enough that she could hear both sides of the conversation, and she smiled as the men traded insults before Andrew got

down to business. When the man on the
other end of the call relayed Jetty's arrival,
she heard the undeniable squeal of Grace's
delight in the background.

Well, that answered that question. He
wasn't lying about Grace, and judging by the
rest of the men's short conversation, she and
her friend would be reunited within the
hour. Things were moving right along. If
everything continued to check out, she'd be
able to give the green light to her people
regarding the safe harbor offer, but she was
still reserving judgment. She would have to
meet the Alpha and see more of the town
after meeting with Grace.

One bite at a time. That was the only way
to eat a whale.

The visit with Grace was all Jetty could
have wished for. Grace was glowing with
happiness, and it was obvious her bear
shifter mate was equally besotted. As the day
dawned bright and beautiful, Grace and Jetty
sat on the deck of Jack and Grace's house,
looking out over the water. Andrew took
Jack a short distance away, to walk along the
beach for a few minutes, letting the ladies
have a few private minutes to themselves.

"I wish you could find the kind of happiness I have, Jet," Grace gushed, truly in love. "Jack is the best man I've ever known. He saved me on more than just the physical level." At this point, Grace's gaze went dark. "The leviathan had its hooks into me on a magical level. I kept trying to go back into the water, right back into its clutches. It was calling me. I've never been so scared in my life, but Jack saved me. He figured a way—with the help of the local shaman—to join his magic to mine. We're truly one now, and I'll never leave him. I love him so much, Jet." Grace's eyes lit from within with the shine of true love.

Jetty was convinced. Between the way Grace gushed over her new guy and the way Jack looked at Grace, the love clear in his open expression, Jetty knew they were meant to be. She hugged her friend, truly happy for her. Finding a mate that matched your heart and soul was every shifter's dream.

Grace insisted on coming into town with Andrew and Jetty later that morning, to introduce her around and show her the sights. Grace had loaned her more presentable clothing, and the four of them took two vehicles—Andrew's convertible and Jack's SUV—down the rough road that led to the apex of the cove, where the town center was laid out.

Grace seemed to be having fun showing off her friend to the people they met as they strolled along Main Street, visiting several art galleries, a souvenir shop, and finally, the much acclaimed bakery. The town's famous bakery was everything Jetty had imagined, and then some. Two of the sisters who owned the place where there and seemed genuinely happy to meet a friend of Grace's. Jetty liked the way they teased Jack and Grace about their newly mated status. It was clear Grace had made good friends in this small town.

They all ate lunch at the bakery, spending an hour and more nibbling on delicious sandwiches and pastries and sipping rich, hot coffee. It was truly one of the nicest meals Jetty had shared with anyone in a long time. She missed this camaraderie, living in the ocean. She missed the simple act of dining out was good friends, talking and laughing.

Life under the waves was great, but it was harsh as well. One always had to be on guard against predators, and communication was more difficult. Oh, Jetty had friends among her hunting party, but it was different underwater. Even her relationship with Grace was different in the sea.

They were much more at ease on land. Able to spend time just enjoying each other's company, without having to be on the lookout at all times. And the company was pretty fantastic too. These bear shifters were polite, funny, and very easy on the eyes. In fact, Jetty hadn't met one person yet, who wasn't tall, athletic, and very attractive.

Living in Los Angeles, she'd been surrounded by beautiful people. Actors and actresses always tried to look their best, and it felt like the prettiest people from around the country all went there, trying to break into show business. It had been hard to compete with some of the bombshells that populated the city. Not that Jetty had low self esteem. She knew she was fit and reasonably attractive, in the mer way…but Dirk the Jerk, and so many of the men she had dated, seemed to want perfection.

Sure as hell, Jetty knew she wasn't perfect. Not by a long shot.

Not that she really wanted to be some plastic, picture perfect version of herself. She was who she was, and she had begun to really like herself over these past years spent in self-discovery, in the ocean. Things were a lot simpler there.

They were just about finished with lunch, when the little bell over the door to the bakery tinkled, indicating a new arrival. The men greeted the newcomer—a powerfully built man with an extremely commanding presence. Introductions were made, and before she realized it, Jetty had met the Alpha bear.

John, as the Alpha insisted she call him, joined them at the table, and more coffee was poured and snacks refreshed. It looked like she was about to have her meeting with the Alpha bear right then and there, which was just as well. Everything Jetty had seen of Grizzly Cove had impressed the hell out of her.

Just this one final thing to tick off her list and she'd have made her decision—in favor of accepting the bears' offer of safe harbor. All she had to do was go back and tell her hunting party, who would then send messengers to the pod. But first, she had to lay out a few things for the bears, so they'd understand the full meaning of their offer.

Drew was listening intently as Jetty got down to business with John. Everything that had happened so far felt really positive. He thought the town had done its best to impress Jetty. And he knew Grace was thrilled to have her friend here. Grace's enthusiasm was obvious and would go a long way toward convincing Jetty that the offer of asylum was real and honest.

Talking with John was the logical next step. He was glad when the Alpha showed up. With any luck, they could get this all wrapped up before dinner, and Jetty would be convinced to come back and stay here while the danger lasted out in the ocean.

If Drew had anything to say about it, he would do his best to convince her to stay much longer than that. Maybe forever. And that wasn't such a scary thought, the longer he was in her presence.

He almost suspected... No. It couldn't be that simple. Nobody found their mate so easily.

Did they?

"So you see, John," Jetty was saying as the conversation turned serious, "my hunting party is just a small part of the larger group." Drew noticed Grace nodding at

Jetty's side, and he tuned into the conversation once more. "The hunting party is one of several that guard and provide for the pod. Our pod consists of a few dozen families. The singles of suitable age and ability form the hunting parties. So the terms need to be made clear. Are you offerings safe harbor to just my hunting party, or will you extend it to the pod?"

"When you say families, you mean children? Mothers. Fathers. Aunts. Uncles. Right?" John seemed to be thinking hard, a frown marring his brow.

"Grandfathers and grandmothers, too, though the mer population has always skewed more toward the female. Males of any age are few and far between," Jetty told them.

John grunted, his bear showing through in the sound. The idea of more females in the area would appeal to all the single men, so that was a plus as far as Drew could see.

"We can't leave them out there to fend for themselves against the leviathan," Jack said, holding hands with Grace. "Not when concentrating our people here is what lured it. We're responsible."

John looked at Drew, seeking his opinion

without words. Drew nodded. They'd always been about protecting the innocent. That was their mission. Always had been. Drew knew the rest of the unit would feel the same.

"It's what we do, John," Drew said. "Our mission has never changed. We protect. It makes our bears happy."

"Yeah," John allowed, sitting back in his chair. "I think we won't get any argument in extending the invitation to the entire pod."

Relief flooded Grace's expression as she put her free hand over Jetty's and squeezed. Jetty smiled, but still looked cautious.

"Thank you, Alpha. It means a lot that you and your people would be willing to do that for us. There are just a few details we need to work out before I can go back and give them this great news."

"Details?" John asked.

"Yeah, like what are they going to wear on land?" Drew thought, starting to warm to the logistical problems. "And where do they come ashore? We have a pretty steady flow of tourists nowadays. We can't have mermaid sightings drawing crackpots up here. It'll have to be discreet."

Jetty laughed at his crackpot joke, but

nodded. "If there could be some sort of structure…like a boathouse or something, where we could surface indoors and clothes could be stored."

"That's perfect," Drew replied, already thinking of possible locations for such a building.

"And we need at least one of the shops to begin stocking more women's clothing. And a bank branch would be awesome too. Our people have ties in the banking industry since we tend to pop out of the water all over the place and need funds in the local currencies. We could probably arrange for a satellite branch to open up here, if you all agree," Grace put in, surprising the heck out of Drew. She was being a lot more forthcoming with information about her people now that Jetty was here.

The women went on planning, and John made a few phone calls to get more of the unit to join them. It looked like this was going to be an all-out effort, and it was important to have all the guys on board from the beginning. One by one, the key individuals arrived at the bakery for an impromptu meeting. Tables were pushed together and coffee served as the planning began in earnest.

As Jetty was introduced and the situation explained, every single guy agreed with the plan. Drew was proud of his buddies. Not one of them even entertained the idea of leaving those mer out there, in danger. Before long, a plan was devised, and work would begin at sunset. The basic structure of the boathouse would go up overnight, with all the guys pitching in. Some of the other things would take a bit more time, but the important point was that things were being set in motion.

Through it all, Drew watched Jetty interact with his friends. The single men mostly found her attractive. Some flirted. Some even issued invitations, which made him want to growl, but she just smiled and remained noncommittal with them all, which made him feel a little better. If she was going to accept an invitation, he preferred it was one of his.

He was planning to throw his hat in the ring—for better or worse—before he'd let her swim away. His bear was having a hard time with the idea that they had to let her go, though he knew she had to communicate what she'd learned to her people. The furry side of him growled at the knowledge that she would have to leave. It wanted to stop her. It wanted to keep her. All to himself.

It was way too early in their relationship—if they even had a relationship—to be thinking things like that. Drew knew his thoughts were a little too possessive. A little too emphatic. A little too primitive. But there it was. Caveman Drew, at your service.

It didn't make a whole lot of sense. He was fighting instincts he didn't fully understand. Animal instincts. The bear was clawing at his insides, trying to get at her, but not to hurt her. No, the bear just wanted to be near her. To rub up against her and stand between her any possible danger.

When the meeting finally broke up, it was nearly dinnertime. They'd spent all afternoon in the bakery, having a marathon planning session. A lot of good points had been raised, and a lot of really solid plans had been set into motion. All in all, Drew was really pleased with the outcome of the day.

The only thing that would make him happier was if he could convince Jetty to stay with him just a little longer. It was selfish, he knew. Every minute she delayed her departure was a minute her people were still in danger. The sooner she spread the news of Grizzly Cove and the welcome that waited here for the mer, the better.

But he'd only just found her. The more he was around her, the more he wanted to be in her presence. He would follow her into the depths of the ocean, if he could. Barring that extreme, he'd try to enjoy the few moments they had left to their fullest.

He couldn't really do that in a crowd. Rather than stick around after the meeting, sharing small talk with his buddies, Drew ushered Jetty out the door, right along with Grace and Jack. Drew stood impatiently as the two mer women said their goodbyes, hoping to avoid any more delay in returning to his home. He had plans, and they were running out of time. She had to leave, but before she did, he wanted to make it clear to her that he was interested. More than interested, actually.

The kiss they'd shared had awakened his primitive side, and the bear wanted her. The human side of him wanted her in his bed, in his life, but the bear wanted to protect her. Always.

But he also didn't want to scare her off. It

was going to be a delicate conversation. One he'd never had with any other female. Jetty was special. More special than she knew.

Jetty was glad when the meeting broke up. She had been very impressed by the bears' willingness to help her people. Their planning and logistics expertise was very apparent, and she felt content to leave preparations in their hands. Grace would oversee things and guide them in the right direction, if necessary, but Jetty had great confidence, after talking with them all at length, that they would create something very special here. As they had, in fact, with their entire town.

Grizzly Cove was pretty amazing. She'd really enjoyed herself today, which was something she hadn't anticipated. She'd figured one town was very much like another, and after LA, a small artists' colony on the rugged part of the Washington coast wouldn't be all that interesting. Boy, had she been wrong.

The place was idyllic. A peaceful slice of Americana dressed up in shifter style. Oh, it wasn't obvious that the town was full of shifters. They still had to keep a low profile.

Humans could wander through at anytime, after all. But the pervasive feeling of the place was one of acceptance and peace. It was like nothing she had ever experienced outside the ocean before.

Certain parts of the Pacific had that same feeling, but they weren't as plentiful as they once had been. The oceans were being damaged in places by pollution and human traffic on the surface, in their giant container vessels, crisscrossing the earth's oceans at will. Humans were everywhere nowadays—even in the deeps.

They weren't that bad, usually, but the idea that Grizzly Cove was populated by a large majority of magical beings made it very attractive. Jetty thought most of her mer friends would fit right in. And a lot of the single women would find dates readily enough with all those hunky single men.

Grizzly Cove was about to be invaded, and they really didn't understand the full power of the tsunami that was going to hit them. Jetty almost laughed, thinking about it as she sat next to Andrew, in the passenger seat of his car. They were heading back to his place. She had an hour or two before her planned departure, and she wanted to spend the time with him.

She'd been happy when he ushered her out of the bakery and suggested going back to his place. She'd liked the people she'd met today, but it was Andrew who really captured her attention. He was so very handsome. And sometimes, he looked so lost. So sad.

That's what had drawn her to his boat, day after day. She'd spied on him, watching him from the water. Wondering what drove him out there, rain or shine. She sensed something in him that called to her to help. To observe and devise a way to heal.

She knew it sounded ridiculous. Even she had a hard time believing the silly thoughts that dashed through her mind at times. Still, the idea refused to let her go. And the more she was around him, the more she talked to him, the more she wanted—no, needed—to find a way to help him. He was in need. She just didn't fully understand what it was he needed.

She'd vowed to figure it out. Maybe not today, but at least she'd made a start. She'd befriended him, deepening their connection today, laying the groundwork. She would work on him until he let her in and allowed her to learn how to soothe him.

Ridiculous, maybe, but it was her goal.

Andrew was too special to leave in pain. Too handsome to ignore. Too honorable to deny.

He pulled the car up in front of his house. From every angle, the structure was absolutely gorgeous. She loved his house, outside and in.

"Do you have to go back right away?" he asked as he opened the door for her.

"It would be best to leave after dark," she replied. "I want to hug the shore as long as possible to stay within the wards, but parts of that path are shallow, and there's a possibility, however slim, that someone could spot me from the air during daylight hours."

"After dark it is, then," he agreed with a merry tone in his voice as they went into his house. "Does that mean I can interest you in some dinner?"

She put one hand over her stomach, thinking about all the delicious pastries she'd eaten at the bakery. Luckily, she had a mer metabolism, which meant she was pretty much always hungry because she burned so many calories swimming all the time. Things were a little different on land, though.

"Maybe in an hour?" she suggested. "I ate a lot at the bakery."

"That works," Drew told her. "I've got some steaks marinating in the fridge. I can fire up the grill, and we can eat out on the deck. That'll help us pass the time. I've also got a nice bottle of wine, if you're interested."

She smiled at him. "I'm definitely interested."

She hoped he understood the full meaning of her words. She didn't want to leave here tonight without at least one more of those stellar kisses of his—or maybe even a whole lot more.

CHAPTER FIVE

Drew bustled around for a bit, setting everything up. He brought out the wine and poured her a glass, insisting she sit down and put her feet up on the oversized chaise he kept out on the deck. He slept in the thing, at times, and knew it was comfortable. He wanted her to feel safe and relaxed while he took care of everything.

He set the grill to warm up and got the steaks out of the fridge in the kitchen, transferring them to the workspace he'd built around the grill. He toasted her with his own glass of wine while he got things going.

"So what do you think of the cove, now that you've had a chance to really look around?" he asked, wanting to make conversation.

The way she was looking at him was making him think things that might just be a tad inappropriate. Or not. He'd try his luck after dinner and see if she was as receptive as he thought. But for now, he was on a mission to feed her before she left. He wanted her to remember how well he took care of her so that she'd want to come back.

"It's beautiful. The waters are still perfect—a safe place to swim and raise young. The pod will appreciate that. We have a few children living in the sea right now, but they're reaching an age where they should probably start learning about life on land too. This looks like a good place for them to do it."

"There aren't a lot of children in town yet, but there is one little girl who would probably love to have some playmates. She's about five years old and a panda shifter." Drew thought of young Daisy, who had come here with her mother after her father had died, back in China.

Daisy was the sweetheart of the town and every heart melted when she held her arms out to be picked up. Daisy and her mother,

Lynn, had known tragedy, but they were slowly healing and making a new life for themselves here in Grizzly Cove.

"A panda? No kidding? She must be absolutely adorable."

Drew smiled. "You have no idea. She's equally cute in either form. And her mother is a force to be reckoned with. I'm actually surprised you didn't get a chance to meet them today. Lynn is usually in town for lunch, since she runs one of the galleries. Remember the one with all the bamboo?"

Jetty laughed. "I should've guessed. Pandas love bamboo, don't they?"

"They do. I was surprised that Lynn wasn't in today, but everyone needs a day off now and again, right?" He put the steaks on the grill, then walked over to refill her wine glass.

Unable to resist her allure, he sat down on the edge of the wide chaise, facing her as they sipped their wine. The mood was intimate. Quiet. Charged.

"What did you think of the town? The people?" he asked over the rim of his wine glass.

"The town is charming. The people..." She paused, seeming to think. "The women were nice, the men, a little intimidating."

"Not to you, surely?" he asked, knowing his Jetty was made of sterner stuff.

She laughed. "No. Not to me. But if you take all those men as a group, I can see where humans—and a lot of Others—would be somewhat intimidated. You're a powerful unit."

"We were the best the Special Forces had to offer. When we were working all together, nothing could stand in our way." He knew he was speaking no less than the truth, and he felt pride in what his friends and he had accomplished.

Of course, he'd been sidelined well before the other guys. Personally, he thought maybe his injury had been the beginning of the end for his team. Right after he almost got blown to bits, the other guys had started thinking seriously about retiring. Oh, they'd brought up the idea once or twice over the years, but after Drew got hurt, it seemed like priorities had changed.

They wouldn't admit to it, but Drew knew. He could put two and two together. While he'd been healing, his team had been starting the process that eventually resulted in Grizzly Cove. He hadn't asked John about it outright yet, but he would one day.

John was a long-term strategist. He always planned things out—years in advance, sometimes. Grizzly Cove was one of those. John had revealed that he'd been quietly buying up the land around here for decades before he was ready to reveal his plan for the town to his men. They'd gone along with it, to a man, which said something about John's leadership and the faith his people had in him.

"Why did you all decide to retire?" Jetty asked, unknowingly opening an old wound.

Drew sighed. He could gloss over it, but for some reason, he wanted her to know the truth.

"In my case, it wasn't a choice. I got blown up by a roadside bomb, and they had to send me back State-side to glue what was left back together." Jetty was frowning, but she didn't say anything, which was good. He wouldn't be able to get it out if she interrupted. "My mom took over my healing, and thanks to her stubbornness and determination, I lived. And I didn't lose any limbs, though that was a close thing, she tells me."

She sat forward, putting her hand over

his, but it felt like she knew not to say anything until he'd finished. They were in tune already.

"I spent months healing from something that would've killed anyone else. Anyone without my mom pulling for them." They both knew that for a shifter to take *months* in healing, the wounds had to be serious. Most shifters healed incredibly fast due to their accelerated metabolisms. "The mental scars were harder to deal with than the physical ones."

"Which is why you seek the peace of the ocean," Jetty whispered, moving closer. Drew didn't object when she reached out and put her arms around him, offering the comfort of her embrace. "I understand that. Perhaps better than anyone here."

She cupped his cheek in her palm and turned his face toward hers. And then, they were kissing. It was a gentle kiss filled with understanding and banked passion that threatened to overtake them given the slightest provocation. Drew had never felt anything like it with any other female. Jetty was special.

Mate special.

He drew back, and she let him go with a

last lingering caress on his cheek. Her touch was like satin, her skin the softest he'd ever known. She was all things good in the world, and his thoughts were quickly racing into very serious territory.

"You'd better turn the steaks," she whispered, her smile inviting at the same time she pushed him away.

But it didn't feel like she was pushing him very far. He just had to rescue dinner, and she'd still be here, waiting for him. Possibly to pick up where they'd left off? He could only hope.

"Yeah." Drew slapped his hands on his thighs in order to keep them off her. She was in charge here, and he had to make that clear. He wasn't some cave bear that couldn't behave himself.

He got up and worked on the steaks until they were done. They both liked their meat cooked medium well, so serving up dinner was an easy thing. She moved over to the table and chairs set up near the grill and took her seat while he served, then took his own chair.

They ate and drank the wine, enjoying each other's company. She talked about the town, asking questions about things and people she hadn't yet discovered, and he enjoyed filling her in on the details. She revealed a bit more about her former life in LA. She'd been a high school teacher and yoga instructor on the side, he was fascinated to learn.

"If we ever set up a school here, you'd have a job, no problem. Big John has plans for this town that are far-reaching. If we get enough families to settle here, he's already discussed looking for teachers who are shifters."

"He's quite the strategist."

"You have no idea."

When they finished eating, Drew tidied things away, refilling Jetty's wine glass as she sat on the big chaise once more, looking out over the beach. The sun was setting on a gray evening, clouds rolling in, as they so often did in this part of the country.

"Looks like rain tonight," Drew observed as he finished clearing things away and came back out to sit with her.

She smiled. "I love water in all its forms."

"So it's not like in that old movie where if the mermaid gets wet, she shifts no matter what?" he challenged, grinning at her over the rim of his glass from much too far away.

He was seated on the foot of the chaise, facing her.

She laughed outright. "No. It's not like that at all. I control the shift. Water isn't necessary to shift, but it *is* necessary to move around once I've got a tail, so it's wiser to wait until I'm in the water to change."

"A wise precaution," he agreed, enjoying the intimate moment as the sun's last rays began to fade.

He scooted a few inches closer to her. When she made no objection, he moved closer still.

She didn't move away or make any other gesture that he could interpret as discomfort. In fact, her eyes had gone soft, her pulse increasing. She seemed as aware of him as he was of her.

"I've never met anyone like you," he whispered, raising one hand to brush a stray lock of hair off her brow. It was so soft. So sensual.

"You've met Grace," she argued with a little grin that told him she was teasing him, and enjoying it.

"You're not like Grace. Not in the important ways. You might both be mer, but you're vastly different women. Grace is a sweetheart, but she doesn't call to me—to my bear—the way you do. The way you have since I first laid eyes on you."

"Your bear likes me?" She swayed forward, coming closer, sliding her arms around his neck.

"Oh, yeah." Drew moved into the embrace, drawing her close. "He likes everything about you. And so does my human side."

"That's really good," she said breathlessly, her mouth only centimeters from his. "Because both sides of my nature have been stuck on you for months now."

Months? He would have pursued that thought, but she closed the gap between them, touching her lips to his.

Like spark to tinder, that was all the encouragement he needed to take things to the next level. Drew kissed her with all the longing inside him, taking her mouth with the deep satisfaction he'd somehow known would be waiting for him in her arms.

She was heaven in his arms, and when she twisted around in his embrace, he went with her. He'd let her steer the ship, if that's what she wanted. Anything. He'd give her anything she wanted.

Jetty liked that her big bad bear was willing to let her take charge a little. She rolled him over onto his back on the wide chaise, planting her hands on his muscular shoulders and one of her knees on either side of his lean hips.

She kissed him the way she'd wanted to for a long time. He had intrigued her ever since she'd first caught sight of him in his little boat, months ago. She had spied on him from the water, watching his rugged face, his perfect body, as he fished.

He'd seemed so sad, at times, she'd almost broken cover to talk with him. At other times, he simply seemed at peace with the ocean—the way she was—which seemed odd to her for a land shifter, but somehow beautiful. And then there were times when he drank all day, to the point where he was talking to the fish he pulled in, his words slurred, the emotional pain in him very close to the surface. At those times, her heart had yearned to go to him, to comfort him, but she could not.

Through it all, there was the attraction. She'd felt drawn to him as she had never before been drawn to another male.

She had known from almost the moment he'd called her name that first day they'd spoken that, somehow, they'd end up here. Not here—on his deck—in particular, but together. Kissing. Exploring. Learning each other's bodies as they had begun to learn each other's minds and personalities.

She liked him even more than she'd thought she would. He was open-minded and caring. Considerate and strong. A warrior with a good heart, from all that she had seen so far. She respected him. And her respect was not something easily earned.

She also had the hots for him, which was why she had taken charge for the moment. She wanted to be an equal partner in this— and in all things they did together. He might as well get a taste of that right now. *Begin as she meant to go on,* and all of that.

Enjoying the feel of his hard body beneath her, she kissed him with all the pent-up longing that had built up over day and weeks…months, even…of watching him. She'd wanted to do this for so very long, and the reality was better than any of her imaginings.

He was so warm under her, his skin radiating heat that spoke to her human side.

She wanted to snuggle up to him forever. She had the fanciful notion that, even in the cold of the ocean, he would keep her warm.

She pulled back slightly, licking at his lips. She wanted to see his expression as she lowered herself over him, making full body contact for the first time. There might be two layers of clothing still between them, but the moment was significant to her. She hadn't been this close to a male since she'd left land years ago. Opening herself up to Andrew like this was something special. She wanted to know it was special to him too.

She met his gaze, watching him carefully as she rubbed herself against him slowly, in imitation of what they'd soon be doing skin to skin, if she had her way. She saw the flare of desire in his eyes, heard the sexy rasp of his breath.

"If you're trying to make me insane with desire, that ship has sailed, my finned beauty." He raised one slightly shaky hand to caress her cheek as she smiled.

"Finned beauty?" She didn't want to admit how much she liked that.

"I've been trying to come up with something original, since you're like no other woman I've ever known. Fair warning—I've got a few more I want to try out." His humor sparked hers, and she had to smile.

"I can't wait to see what you've come up with." All the while, she kept up her subtle torture, squirming against him, rubbing their bodies slowly together.

She kissed him again, the passion rising like the tide.

Within moments, she was pushing at his clothing, nearly mindless with the need that had come up so suddenly, it nearly stole her breath. The tempest was upon her, and all she could think of was getting him naked.

Thankfully, he was having a lot more luck undressing her than she was with him. Within moments, she was bare, but he was still clothed. It wasn't fair!

A keening sound startled her, and she realized it had come from her. The frenzy was building, and she needed him to be naked. And then, she needed him to be inside her. Simple as that.

Andrew seemed to know what she needed. While she fretted, he was busy undoing buttons and zippers, and tearing fabric when necessary to get them both naked. She felt more and more skin against hers, which made her smile, calming some of the frenzy down to a more manageable state.

They lay there for just a few minutes, side by side, skin to skin, kissing as the night deepened and a soft rain began to fall.

"Do you want to go inside?" Andrew asked at one point, not rushing things, treating her like she was precious to him, charming her with his care. "Are you cold?"

She had to laugh. Looking into his eyes, she let one eyebrow lift. "Dude." Some of her Southern Californian roots were showing through in her words. "I live in the ocean. I love water, and I don't chill easily, even in human form." Then she thought about his comfort. "But if you want to take this inside…"

She lifted away but his strong arms hauled her back. "Not on your life," he protested, laughing with her. "I've got you exactly where I want you. A little rain won't hurt either of us. We're shifters. We're strong. And we like nature, in all her moods. Right?"

"I couldn't agree more. Now, where were we?" She straddled him again, bringing her core into shockingly fast contact with his hard length. "Oh, yeah. We were about to get down to business."

"I like the sound of that," he enthused,

lifting his big hands to cup her breasts.

He knew just how to rub her nipples to make her squirm in delight, and his hands—his whole body—was so warm. He was like a furnace. A living, breathing, hard-bodied furnace. Yum.

She'd been primed for him from their first kiss on the boat. The talking and dinner had only made her want him more. She'd been starved for this kind of male companionship, being out at sea for so long, and she didn't want to wait another minute to find out what it would be like to be with a bear shifter. *Her* bear shifter.

Jetty hadn't lusted after any other sort of shifter before, though she had run across a few in passing, years ago. They'd been average. Like her, only with different animal spirits. But this one…this big badass bear…had intrigued her from the moment she'd first seen him.

Now that she had him in her clutches, she wasn't about to let him get away. Although, it was sort of laughable to think that she could overpower him. Even with all the strength of her mer half, he was still male and still a whole lot stronger than her physically. She knew, though, deep down in her heart, that he'd never use that incredible strength against her.

If anything, he would use it to protect her. He didn't fully realize yet how little she actually *needed* protecting, but it was a sweet thought.

As the soft rain coated their bodies in cool moisture that did nothing to cool their ardor, she adjusted her position until she felt the tip of him at her entrance. There was no need for barriers between them. They were shifters. They were in rhythm with the ocean, in tune with the woodlands. They didn't carry human diseases, and she knew when she was entering a fertile time. She still had a ways to go for that, so this joining could be stress free and natural.

She moved slowly downward, the lubrication of the rain and the natural slickness of her body brought him into her by slow degrees. She held his gaze as she accepted his thickness. He was masterfully built. Hard, wide and long. Just as she liked it.

The intimacy of looking into his beautiful brown eyes as they came together nearly stole her breath. This was why the Goddess had given mer a human form. So they could experience this amazing oneness with another being. The union of bodies, hearts and souls…

But such romantic thoughts were ripped from her mind as he lifted his hips slightly, coaxing her to take more of him faster. So he wanted to play, did he?

Jetty leaned downward and nipped his lip, bringing forth a sexy growl from his inner bear. She liked that sound. It made her want more.

She took all of him, seating him fully within her, gasping as he bottomed out, sending little tingles of pleasure all up and down her body. She'd never felt such magical sensations…and they'd only just begun.

"You feel so damn good," he whispered.

She looked deep into his eyes and had to agree. "Right back at'cha, big boy."

That seemed to surprise a laugh out of him, right as she began moving. The laugh turned into a rumbling growl of satisfaction as she slid up and down on his shaft, taking them both to new heights of pleasure.

She started out slow, but things quickly escalated to something hard and fast and hot, hot, hot. Little sounds came from her mouth, and he was growling down deep in his chest, turning her on even more. She liked the sounds her bear made when he was inside her. They were an aphrodisiac in themselves.

He grabbed her hips, and she let him guide her the last few deep, quick thrusts until she was crying out, ecstasy hitting her, sweeping her up in the torrent that went on and on. At some point, she felt him join her in climax, his voice ripping her name from his chest in a throaty growl.

Oh, yes! That was what she wanted to hear. Music to her ears.

The orgasm lasted longer than anything she could remember. It was like a bunch of tiny climaxes all rolled into one. A new experience that threatened to shatter her perceptions of reality and probably ruin her for all other men.

She collapsed on his chest, enjoying the way he drew her close, cuddling her as their breathing started to slow. There were no words for this moment. It was too perfect. Too exceptional. Too…almost…sacred.

Words would come later. After they'd both had a chance to catch their breaths.

Words of goodbye—because she had a

mission to fulfill. She still had to go back to her people tonight and tell them her findings about Grizzly Cove.

For now, though, they could cuddle on the chaise lounge. Revel in the aftershocks of their passion. Be wrapped in Mother Nature's misty rain, dewing their skin like a blessing from above. For now…Jetty could bask in the arms of her lover.

A long, long time later, Jetty rolled off him, moving to his side in preparation for pulling herself away from his embrace. It was going to be hard to tear herself away. One of the most difficult things she'd ever done. She almost wanted to forget all about her duty to her people…but she couldn't. That wasn't her. She was responsible for so much. People were depending on her, and she couldn't let them down.

"I don't want to leave," she admitted. "But I'll have to go soon."

"I wish you didn't have to go either." He ran his fingers up and down her arm, making her shiver in pleasure.

"But I have to," she reminded him.

"I know, but I can still wish it were otherwise, can't I?" He sent her a sleepy smile. "At least stay the night."

"But I have to swim out under cover of darkness."

"Not if I drive you out there on my boat. We could spend the night here and leave at dawn. Or before dawn, if you'd rather. That's my normal routine, so nobody would be surprised. What do you say, my cute little fishy?"

"Cute little fishy?" She wrinkled her nose, smiling.

"No? How about saline sweetheart?" She shook her head. "Kelp maiden? Oceanic beauty?" He tried several of the pet names he'd warned her about, and she dissolved in giggles as his tone took on a more dramatic flair with each new selection.

She shook her head as he persisted, loving his teasing. Above all, she loved a man who could make her laugh.

"How about Jetty, my jewel?" He kissed her, his voice dropping low. "The rarest pearl in the oyster of my life." His tone was less teasing now, more serious as passion seemed to roll over them both again.

When he let her up for air, she smiled lazily into his gaze. "I like that last one."

"My pearl." He nodded. "That's the truest one. You're rare and precious.

Beautiful and magical."

He kissed her again, and they were swept up in the glory of being with each other, the soft, misty rain slicking their skin as they joined together once more.

CHAPTER SIX

Getting ready to take Jetty out on the boat was hard the next morning. They'd spent the night in bliss, dozing only to wake and make love again. Drew had never experienced another night like it in his life. It was near perfect. The only thing marring the moment was the fact that he'd have to let her go this morning.

And it wasn't just letting her go. It was letting her go back out there—into danger. That's what was really killing him.

In a break from his normal, lonely routine, Jetty helped him make sandwiches in the dark well before dawn. She laughed and joked with him as she smeared jelly and peanut butter on bread, licking her fingers and his mouth with equal gusto when they paused for a passionate kiss.

She went back to making sandwiches, a little breathless, but smiling. He loved watching her move. She brought light and joy into his home that hadn't been there…ever.

"Mm. I haven't had PB&J in years," she told him, making two of the gooey sandwiches and putting them in plastic baggies.

Drew worked at her side, frying up the few eggs he had in the house and putting them on bread to make egg sandwiches. They didn't have too much more time here before they'd have to head out on the boat, but he enjoyed every second he had in her presence.

Whether they were in bed or in the kitchen, just being with her made him feel…happy. Drew paused as the thought struck him. He hadn't been truly happy in a very long time, so it was hard to name the feeling Jetty stirred in him, but he had to admit, he thought it felt like happiness. Something he hadn't really expected to find again in this lifetime.

He'd seen too much. Done too much as a soldier. He'd been the witness—and sometimes the cause—of human suffering. His heart hadn't been able to stand much more, which was why he'd been glad when he'd retired. Leaving the service when he had...well...it had almost been too late.

Drew had spent a lot of time thinking since rejoining his unit here. He'd sought the peace of the ocean, but it didn't always fulfill him. Not like having Jetty near. He was fast learning that having her nearby went a long way toward curing what ailed him—emotionally, psychologically, and even spiritually.

She was light when he was in darkness. All she had to do was just be there, and he could finally see everything that had been missing in him for so very long.

But she had to leave. Soon.

She was going into danger, and he was going to deliver her into the arms of the beast. It didn't sit well. Not at all.

"Jetty." He spun to face her after turning off the stove. He'd finished with the eggs, and they were nearly packed and ready to go. He waited until he had her full attention before speaking further. "When we get out there today…" He walked a step closer to her, holding her gaze, trying to figure out how to express himself. "I'm going to stay on the water all day. If at all possible, I'd be happy to bring you and any of your people who want to come with us, back here tonight."

She moved toward him, her gaze troubled. "They may take a while to decide. I can't guarantee they'll want to come at all. And if they do decide to come ashore, I don't know when that'll be."

He closed the distance between them, taking her into his arms. "That's okay. I'll be on the water every day from dawn to dusk, waiting for you, if I have to. I want you safe, my pearl." He whispered the last bit, just before crushing her lips with his.

This kiss was one of longing and fear. He sought to imprint himself on her so that she would remember him and have a reason to return.

Drew felt so damned powerless in this situation. He'd just found everything he'd ever wanted, but he had to give it up. And he didn't know if he'd ever see her again.

She could go out into the deeps and run into something terrible where he wouldn't be able to help her. She could be killed, and he'd never know what had happened to her. He could lose her before they ever really got a chance to be together.

One stolen night was not enough. His bear—and his human heart—demanded more. He wanted it all.

She was his mate.

That earth-shattering thought was the only thing that could make him release her. He staggered back a step, trying to process the thoughts that had come straight from his instinctual knowing. The reservoir of magic in his soul—the place where the bear spirit lived—guided him told him the truth of it. After only one beautiful night with her, he knew for certain that Jetty Silver of the mer was his mate.

Sweet Mother of All.

Andrew released her, an odd expression on his face. That kiss had been pretty spectacular, but then again, every experience she'd had with him had been memorable. He was like no other man she'd ever known, and she regretted having to cut this short, but she had to get back out there and pass on her findings to her people. They were counting on her.

She turned back to the small cooler and closed the lid. They had plenty of sandwiches. She'd eat one or two before she left the boat, but she'd leave the rest for him, feeling a certain mer-ish satisfaction in knowing that she'd helped provide a meal for him, even when she wasn't around to watch him eat it.

Providing food for the others was part of her duties as a member of a hunting party. It was part of her instinct, and her pleasure. She liked hunting and was darn good at it, if she did say so herself. She felt satisfaction in providing for the weaker or less skilled of her people, especially the elders and the tadpoles. She felt joy when she helped others, even in small ways.

Her mother had always said it was because she was a nurturing soul. Jetty admitted that was true, but that wasn't all of it. She was also a warrior. A protector. She didn't see a problem with the way those two inclinations fit together. She was an Alpha female, protecting her pod while nurturing them. Sorta like the mer version of how she imagined a mama grizzly would be. The thought made her smile as she finished packing up the second cooler with ice and drinks.

She noticed Andrew hadn't added any beer to this cooler today. She knew from observing him that he usually drank a local microbrew when he fished, but there was a conspicuous absence of the long, dark bottles in his cooler today. Instead, there were more sensible choices—sports drinks, plain water and even a few sweet, fizzy soft drinks. He was also capping off a big thermos filled with rich, dark coffee when she turned around.

It was super sweet of him. He wanted to stay alert while she was out there with him. That much was obvious.

All packed up, she went over to give him a hug and a kiss. His actions spoke of care and concern, and touched her deeply. When she backed away, he let her go, a bewildered expression on his handsome face.

"What was that for?" he asked in that deep growl that made her lady parts tingle.

"For the pop. I love orange fizz," she teased him, gesturing toward the ice chest with the drinks.

"Well, if I'd known that was all it took to get a kiss, I'd have dragged out my secret stash of fizzy drinks sooner." He looped his arms around her waist again and pulled her in for another devastating, laughter-filled kiss.

He really was the easiest man to be with that she'd ever met. Everything with him was simple. Basic. Delicious and fun, while also meaningful and...real.

He was *real*. That was the crux of it. No pretense. He was as you saw him, with no lies and no subterfuge. Not like the last guy she'd been serious with.

Dirk the Jerk had been an actor. His entire life was a role. He'd never felt a genuine emotion for her, and everything he'd told her was just to advance his own goals of getting her to do what he wanted.

She'd been sick of the lies. Sick of the dishonesty of it all.

With Andrew, that was all over. He was true blue in every sense of the word. Everything he'd told her had turned out to be not only true, but magnificently so. So far, he'd never lied to her, and she got the feeling he never would. Something inside her unfurled and dared to extend a little tendril of trust to him. Little by little, she was growing attached to the bear who was very close to stealing her heart.

But it was time to go. Her mood dropped. She didn't want to go. For the first time in her memory, she wasn't looking forward to putting the human world behind her and embracing the freedom of her mer side.

Now that meant something. Something profound. Something she wasn't ready to contemplate just yet.

"We'd better get going," she whispered

The ride out of the cove was calm, but there was definitely the scent of a brewing storm in the air. The misty rain of the night before had stopped, but it felt like the calm before another band of weather—probably heavier rain—came through.

The weather above didn't impact those below the waves too much, unless it got really violent. The absence of direct sun made things a little darker. A little more mysterious. But then, after a certain depth, things were always dark and mysterious in the underwater world.

Jetty watched Andrew pilot the craft out toward the open sea. He was so handsome she just enjoyed watching him move, his gaze intent on the instruments and the horizon, his muscles shifting as he worked the various controls. There was so much more to him than his looks, though. She'd learned that over the past hours.

He was a man of emotion and depth. One with scars, to be sure, but he was still a being of light, working toward making his life, and the lives of those around him, better. It was a worthy goal, that expressed itself in the town and the people in it. As she'd assessed the town, she'd also made discoveries about the man next to her. She liked everything she'd seen about both.

"Is there a particular area you'd like me to aim for?" he asked, looking from his charts to her as the sun began to rise behind them, kissing the dark sky with orange and red. It looked like an angry sky. It would definitely rain later.

Jetty didn't want to lead him straight to the pod, but she felt confident enough in him now to give him the general region her hunting party patrolled. She moved closer to him, reaching across his chest to point to an area on the chart where shoals of fish usually gathered this time of day.

"This is the most likely spot for my

hunting party right now." Andrew frowned, not even commenting on the way she stroked his muscular chest as she withdrew her hand. That he didn't respond to her teasing aroused her concern. "What is it? What's wrong?"

"Hopefully nothing," he replied, turning the ship's wheel to take them toward the area she'd indicated. "But my spidey sense is telling me we're heading for trouble." He looked at the sonar screen and then back at the chart before meeting her gaze again. "Remember when I told you I could sense where the creatures were congregating and steer clear?"

A chill ran down her spine. "You mean...?"

"They're right about where you pointed, Jetty." He didn't try to sugar-coat his words, but told her outright, which she appreciated. "If your people are there, they might be in trouble."

"They're there. That's our primary fishing ground, and we go there most days at about this time. We've never had a problem before."

"Well, today, they're going to find more than just fish waiting for them, unless I'm totally wrong... But I have to warn you, I'm never wrong about this kind of thing." His expression darkened and he poured on the speed.

The boat cut through the dark water, now tinged with the red of the sunrise peeking through a small band of open sky behind them. The rest of the heavens were covered in gray, the horizon still dark and forbidding.

Jetty held on as the boat leapt to life. A sense of urgency came over her, impressing her from Andrew's serious demeanor.

"What can I do to help?" she asked, worrying, scanning the horizon as they got closer. She thought she saw a disturbance on the surface up ahead, but they were still too far out.

"I'm extending my shields, but be ready to help anyone who needs it out of the water and onto the boat. I can shield them better if they're closer to me." He began hitting different controls, slowing and turning slightly. She trusted that he knew what he was doing. "I can see the big guy. He's moving this way."

He pointed to the chart again, and she realized the leviathan was heading directly toward their fishing grounds—and probably smack-dab into the middle of her hunting party. Andrew's eyesight must be a lot better than hers. Then again, he was a land shifter. Vision was more important on land than underwater.

"Can we get to them before it does?" she whispered, fearing for her friends.

"Just about. I think." He adjusted course and Jetty knew they were almost there. "Thing is, I can hide the magic, but I can't hide our physical presence. If it can see us, it might be interested enough to attack, even if it doesn't sense magic. We'll have to take our chances if your people are there."

"What about the smaller ones? The minions?"

"They seem to scout ahead for the big guy," he said, his frown deepening. "They might already be there, engaged with your people."

"Sweet Mother of All," she swore, praying silently that her friends would be all right.

"Almost there. If there's any way you can get your friends' attention, go for it. Warn them."

Jetty nodded and ran to the bow of the ship, leaning out over the water, looking for signs of her hunting party. They were so close now. She should be able to see something as Andrew slowed the boat, allowing it to drift to a standstill. They were there.

She shucked her clothes and dove head first into the water. Her shift came almost instantaneously, as did her awareness of trouble in the water. Signals were flying between the mer. They were under attack!

Jetty began broadcasting her own signals—squeals and clicks that were mostly too high frequency for human hearing that formed the mer language. She shouted above the din for her hunting party to rally to her. She had a boat. She had a way to protect them from the even bigger evil that was already approaching.

She could see them now. All four members of her party were fighting with one of the smaller creatures. Sirena got up close to it, blinding the hideous thing with her spear, but suffering the crushing grip of the creature's tentacles. The other three slashed at the many arms of the creature, blood flowing freely from both the creature and Sirena before they finally freed her, just as Jetty caught up to them.

She motioned for them to follow her, and thankfully, they didn't argue. Beth supported Sirena, who was in bad shape, while Janice and Marla swam guard. The blinded creature didn't follow, but the blood was attracting too many predators. It was time to leave.

Jetty led them to the stern of Andrew's boat, peeking her head above water to find that he was waiting for her, the back hatch open. She bounded out of the water, unable to guard without a weapon and needing to lead the way for the others. They didn't know him. They wouldn't come aboard his ship unless she was there to guide them.

She shifted quickly, standing by the hatch to show the others the way. The other three helped lift Sirena. It was obvious she was in great pain. Bones were broken, and she was bleeding all over the deck.

Andrew helped lift her as gently as he could, placing her on a collection of seat cushions he'd arranged on the deck for her as the others bounded aboard the way Jetty had. Their weapons made a clatter on the deck, and they all regarded him with suspicion, but thankfully, they seemed to look to Jetty for leadership, now that Sirena was incapacitated.

As was only right. Jetty was second-in-command of the hunting party. If Sirena was hurt, it was up to Jetty to lead.

"Everybody, this is Andrew. He's a bear shifter, and he can shield our magic from the leviathan, which is…" She looked around, her jaw dropping open when she saw the enormous tentacles of the creature just breaking the surface behind them. The big guy, as Andrew called it, had just discovered its injured minion.

A sound unlike any Jetty had ever heard bellowed from the creature, hurting her with the sheer volume and intensity of the frequencies it screamed. All the mer covered their ears, though it did little to help. She looked at Andrew, tears in her eyes from the pain of that sound, and he sprang into action.

"Time to go," he muttered, his deep tones comforting as her senses were bombarded by frequencies he couldn't hear. He was back in the wheelhouse, the boat underway in less than ten seconds, heading back toward Grizzly Cove.

But their passage didn't go unnoticed. The giant leviathan was in pursuit.

Jetty made sure her friends were secure.

The three able-bodied mer were watching over Sirena, trying to stop the bleeding and holding her steady as the boat rocked wildly. Jetty then headed for the wheelhouse to see if there was anything she could do to help. The giant leviathan was right behind them.

Halfway to the wheelhouse, Andrew suddenly dropped anchor and turned the rudder, causing the boat to list hard to port, swinging around, out of the path of the monster. The acrobatic move also nearly swept Jetty off her feet. Sonova...

"Will you warn me next time you plan to do something dangerous?" she screeched at him, regaining her footing.

She marched right up to him in the open hatch to the wheelhouse, and stood her ground, while the leviathan sailed right on past them. With any luck, that maneuver had done the trick.

Drew couldn't help himself. Despite the frantic situation, he cupped her neck and drew her in for a smacking kiss. They didn't have time for it, but he needed to feel her lips against his.

"I promise," he said, grinning as he released her. "See to your friends. I'll get us the hell out of here."

He turned back to the controls, but he hadn't even touched them when he heard a horrendous snap that reverberated through the length of the boat. Everything shuddered for a moment, and he had to think hard about what might've happened below decks. None of the alarms were going off, so they weren't taking on water...yet. Something else must've... Leaning out over the side of the vessel, he realized what had happened.

Worse news, the leviathan had turned and was coming toward them again. Drew's dangerous pivot hadn't worked.

"That fucking beast just snapped my anchor chain," he growled, already forming a plan in his mind as he went for the bow, where the remainder of the chain dangled off the side of the boat. "Jetty! Get everyone down flat on the deck. I'm going to do something dangerous."

Damned if Jetty didn't grin at him. "Thanks for the warning."

"Hey, I promised, didn't I?" He sent her a wink, loving that she was as adventurous as him.

Calling on all the strength of his bear, he heaved the remnant of the massive anchor chain around his shoulders, having released it from its tether to the boat completely. Now he had a heavy length of chain he could use to keep the leviathan busy while they beat a retreat—if he could find the strength to wield it as he planned.

Drew chanted a prayer for strength, digging deep into the things his mother had tried to teach him about his innate magic and the power of the Goddess. He knew the Mother of All would be his ally against the forces of evil, and the creature waving its tentacles around wildly above the surface of the water as it searched for the injured mer was definitely evil.

He chanted as he began to slowly swing the chain, letting out slack as the massive links whistled through the air. He'd climbed to the top of the wheelhouse to get the maximum clearance. He'd have one shot at this—if that. A million things could go wrong with this plan, but he only needed to buy time for their escape.

He prayed as he'd never prayed before and waited for his moment, swinging the huge chain with greater and greater velocity. His concentration was total. He had to tie up as many tentacles as possible with his one and only throw. The longer the monster had to mess with the chain, the longer they'd have to make their escape.

Time slowed. All sound paused. The golden moment came, and Drew knew the exact moment to release the chain. It spun out from his hands, twisting and turning as it flew to its target.

Only when it hit, wrapping around every tentacle that showed above water—which were too numerous to count—did time start up again. There was no time for triumph. Drew had to get his precious cargo out of there with all possible haste.

He jumped off the roof of the wheelhouse, thanking the Goddess as he went, for Her aid. He'd felt Her with him, guiding him, lending him Her magnificent strength. He'd had a spiritual moment up there, on top of his boat, but he didn't have time to savor it. Later, he promised himself. Later, he'd examine what had happened. Maybe talk it over with his mom. Try to figure out what it meant.

Right now, he had to get them the hell out of Dodge.

He somersaulted into the wheelhouse, finding Jetty already there. She gunned the throttle when he gave the nod, and together, they steered them away from the leviathan, heading straight for the safety of the wards surrounding Grizzly Cove.

CHAPTER SEVEN

Jetty moved back and turned over the running of the boat to its master. She only knew the basics. Andrew was the expert here, and she deferred to his skill.

He'd been absolutely amazing to this point. She doubted anyone else could have gotten them out of such a tight spot. She kept glancing out the window, watching the leviathan grow smaller as it remained stationary, struggling with the massive anchor chain that Andrew had somehow managed to toss as if it were made of plastic.

She knew shifters were strong. Bears were probably among the most powerful of the land-based shifters, but this was something even she hadn't expected. She'd have to ask him how he managed it, but she sensed the answer was going to be something rather esoteric. Just for a moment there, while she'd watched him swing that incredibly heavy chain, she saw a magical glow about his person. A sacred glow.

She knew his mother was a priestess. Maybe a little of that had rubbed off on her son? Stranger things had happened. She'd just witnessed some of the strangest events of her life, in fact. At this point, she'd be seeing unicorns and dragons next.

"How are you holding up?" she asked him quietly, knowing he was expending a lot of magical energy in keeping his shield up after the physical—and probably magical—exertion of throwing that chain.

"I'm fine," he answered, though she could see the tight set to his lips that meant he was either in pain, concentrating hard, or both. Probably both, she decided. "You could call ahead. Maybe get the doc to be ready for us."

"On the radio?" She gestured toward the marine radio that was standard equipment in every boat.

"Nah. Don't want every mariner that

might be in range listening in. Use my phone." He unclipped a somewhat bulky phone from his belt and flipped it open, hitting a speed dial number before handing it to her. "That's the town doctor. Just tell him who you are and what happened. I can't talk to him and keep all this going."

All this, meaning the shield and the escape, she figured. He had to be under quite the magical strain, and she didn't want to add to his burden. Plus, she was happy to be part of the rescue in even just this small way.

When a male voice answered the ringing on the other end of the line, she did as Andrew had asked, explaining the situation. Andrew confirmed when asked that he'd aim for the bait shop dock, which was closer to town—and the doctor's office—than his private dock.

The doctor said he'd be waiting, with help. Jetty thanked him and hung up, returning what she now realized was a satellite phone to Andrew. He took it without comment and replaced it on his hip, his concentration on the path in front of them.

"How far to the ward?" she asked quietly.

"Not too far now."

"I don't see any sign of pursuit. The creature seemed good and stuck in that chain. I watched it as long as I could, and I didn't see it moving except to struggle against the binding," she told him.

"That's good," was his only comment.

"Good?" She couldn't help the incredulous tone in her voice. "That's freaking awesome!" She'd tried to contain her enthusiasm until they were completely out of danger, but had to say something. What he'd done... It was straight up amazing. "You saved us."

"Not yet," he argued, keeping his eyes on the path ahead, his concentration near total. "But I'm about to. We're almost to the wards. If we're going to face opposition, it'll be right about here."

She held her breath, but they sailed through with no problem. She knew they were safe the moment the tension in his shoulders eased just the tiniest bit. The strain on him to keep up the shield was easier now. The wards would protect them, even if his shield slipped somehow.

She saw the entrance to the cove and felt a tear trickle down her face. She'd never been so happy to see land.

"Go tell your friends they're safe," he told her gently. "It won't be long now to the dock, and we can get help for their injuries."

She nodded, unable to speak through the emotion clogging her throat. She turned to the deck where her hunting party was laid out like the catch of the day, some bleeding, some still in mer form, some shifted to human, wearing whatever cloth came to hand as they tended the others injuries. She dug right in and helped, finding every last stitch of clothing Andrew had on board and distributing it to those who could use it. She also found items that could be used for first aid and did her best to help where needed.

Before she knew it, they were docking, and there were a host of bear shifters waiting to aid them. Thank the Goddess.

The scene on the dock was a little chaotic, but they managed to get the injured mer woman off the boat without causing her further difficulties. Her three friends went with her, insisting on watching over the one they called Sirena while the town doctor had a look at her injuries. Drew was just as glad to see the others go. As long as Jetty stayed with him, he was content.

When the injured woman had been removed to the doc's capable hands, John came out onto the dock to have a few words. He was frowning, but Drew had seen that expression before. It wasn't the angry frown—which was more like a scowl. This was the concerned frown of a leader who hated to see his people, or those they were trying to protect, in harm's way.

Drew walked over to John, Jetty at his side. John held out his hand for a quick shake and nodded to Jetty in a polite, if distracted, way.

"What happened out there, Drew?" John asked without preamble. Drew knew it was time for the debrief—even though they were still standing on the dock.

"I was attempting to drop Jetty off when I sensed the leviathan approaching the area where her people were fishing. One of the smaller ones attacked first. The ladies managed to fight free before the big one showed up." Drew said succinctly. "If you want to hear the whole sordid tale, come aboard. I can offer you peanut butter and jelly sandwiches and pop." Drew smiled, knowing how far from his normal diet of cold cuts and beer that sounded.

Even John was surprised into a laugh, though he shook his head. "Your boat will be okay here for a while, right?" The Alpha didn't wait for an answer. "How about I buy you two breakfast over at the bakery?"

What followed was an impromptu meeting of the inner circle of their old unit. Sheriff Brody was there, as was his deputy, Zak. The town lawyer, Tom, showed up too. All three were mated—one to each of the sisters who owned the bakery.

John's new mate, Ursula, was waiting for them when they arrived at the bakery, having already commandeered the largest of the tables. She was sitting there, already drinking coffee while the other women set out a large breakfast.

"I guess you had already planned on breakfast for the mated couples this morning," Drew observed.

"It's something the ladies like to do every week or two." John shrugged as he answered. "But it'll serve our purposes. We need to know the details of what happened, so we can better assess the threat and prepare our defenses."

"I know the drill," Drew replied, being sure to keep Jetty at his side. She'd met most of these people at various times yesterday, but being the focus of questioning by such a gathering had to be a little intimidating. "Are you up to this?" Drew asked her, pulling her aside as the others added two chairs to the big table, making room for the newcomers.

"Of course," Jetty surprised him by saying. He looked deep into her eyes, and what he found there gave him a boost of energy. His woman was strong. He shouldn't have doubted her. "They need to know, and there's nothing I can do for Sirena that the others aren't already doing. I do want to go sit with her, though, when this is over. Is that okay?"

"Of course it is." Drew brushed his lips across hers, not caring that everyone was probably watching them. He just had to kiss her. She was such an amazing person…and she was all his. Whether she realized it yet or not.

This morning's adventure had settled it. If there had been any shadow of a doubt about it before, the matter was closed now. She was perfect for him in every way. A woman of sprit and courage. A woman of adventure and heart. His heart had almost stopped when she dove into the ocean after her friends, but he couldn't have been prouder of her. She was his mate.

Drew noticed the raised eyebrows when they joined the others around the big table, but he said nothing. He let the fact that he was holding Jetty's hand speak for itself. Let the others figure it out on their own. He was staking his claim—publicly.

Now, as to whether or not Jetty felt the same…the jury was still out. He had high hopes that, with time and exposure, she would come to love him as much as he already loved her.

And, yes, he was in love with her. She was his mate. Every new facet of her personality he discovered only made him love her more. Telling her, though… That was going to be the tricky part. The last thing he wanted was to scare her off by going too fast.

He'd have to take his time. Get her used to him. Do everything he could to make her want to be with him. And then…he might be able to test the waters and see if she could return his feelings. It was a scary thought, but then, he'd faced down armies of enemy soldiers in his time. Hell, he'd even faced the leviathan with nothing more than a broken anchor chain in his hands. He would manage this. Somehow.

The meeting went on for more than an hour. Jetty told her part of the story, explaining what had taken place beneath the waves in detail to her rapt audience. Drew found he couldn't let go of her hand. He needed the reassurance of feeling her skin against his, to know that she was with him and out of danger.

What she described made him want to growl. When she mentioned that she'd been unarmed—when apparently, she usually *was* armed with a spear at the very least—he wanted to roar. She'd been down there by herself, facing that thing unarmed, while he sat powerless above the surface.

Just thinking of it now made his bear pace inside his skull. The frustration and fear he'd felt at the time had no doubt taken several years off his life.

But she'd made it back to him alive and well. For that, he paused to send a silent prayer of thanks heavenward, to the Mother of All, who must surely have been watching over them all today.

And the day had really only just started.

Jetty was eager to get over to the doctor's

office and see how Sirena was doing as the meeting with the bear leadership wound down. Andrew hadn't let go of her hand once through the long meeting, which she appreciated. She was still shaken up over what had happened out in the ocean.

Oh, she wouldn't let a little case of nerves interfere if she needed to take action. She was a huntress, after all. But she did like the small comfort of his grip on her hand that said without words that he was there for her. That someone was in her corner, willing to lend his support.

That was a new feeling for her. She'd felt alone for a long time—even surrounded by her hunting party, who were all like siblings to her after so long working together. She thought she recognized the same camaraderie among the men of Grizzly Cove. She asked Andrew about it as they walked from the bakery, at the apex of the cove, to the doctor's office, which was at the end of Main Street.

He told her about how the core group of bear shifters were all ex-Special Forces military men. How they'd served together for many years, and all retired around the same time, congregating around their commanding officer and Alpha, John.

"Sirena is our leader, though I guess that title carries a little less weight than Alpha. She's the leader of our hunting party, but we all come under the pod's leadership too. Our society, though...it's more relaxed than land-dwelling shifters. Probably because the distances we cover are so huge. Our hunting party ranges up and down the coast, while the pod proper is much farther out at sea."

"How does that work? I mean, don't you have to bring back your kills for the larger group? Isn't that why you go out hunting for them?"

He seemed truly interested, so she explained more.

"There are many hunting parties, and part of the work is hunting and providing for the pod, but it's also security. We patrol the coast. Other hunting parties patrol other areas. We all return to the pod at organized intervals with our catch and to exchange news and clarify orders from the pod leadership. Our patrol areas get changed every now and again. Sometimes, a hunting party will ask to be reassigned closer or farther from the pod for personal reasons, and they do their best to accommodate. We try to live in harmony with each other as much as possible, but occasionally conflicts do arise."

She didn't want to go into exactly how those rare conflicts were settled just yet. She didn't think he was ready to know just how violent life in the pod could be at times. Although…if anyone would understand those battles for dominance, she thought another shifter might. She just didn't know enough about their rituals and habits to know for sure yet, though she was learning.

"The other part of our duty—the main part—is security. We wanted the coastal patrol because we wanted to be outliers. We sought the peace of the ocean, but didn't want to get involved in the pod politics and power struggles. Most of us in Sirena's hunting party are loners of one type or another, and we like being on land occasionally. In fact, we all grew up on land, unlike the true pod-dwellers who raise their kids in the ocean. Sirena lets us go ashore to phone our parents, siblings and friends whenever we want, which is something the others don't really approve."

"How do you manage it? There aren't many towns along this stretch of coast."

He seemed really interested and a little concerned, as if he realized the dangers they faced each time they came ashore. Maybe he did. Andrew had proven himself an insightful man, and he had to understand the problems of shifting from one form to another.

"Each of us has a cache somewhere. In my case, I've got a waterproof knapsack containing a small tent, some clothing, hiking boots, a prepaid cell phone and a solar charger, stashed in some rocks a little way down the coast. The only approach is from the water and it's hidden well enough that no casual observer is going to find it. If I go there at night, nobody is likely to see me shift and dress. And, if I somehow run into someone on land, I'll pretend to be a hiker."

"I'm impressed," Andrew said as they walked along toward the doctor's office. "But, pardon me for saying, it sounds kind of lonely."

"Yeah." She agreed with him. "It can be. But I call my friends and family, then maybe sleep under the stars and eat some land food. Camp a little. It's peaceful."

"Dangerous too. A female alone, out in the wilderness." He frowned.

She turned to meet his gaze, challenge in her tone. "A huntress. Hunting. Armed and dangerous and able to go fish and escape to the ocean where any pursuit cannot follow."

"If you can make it to the water," he challenged.

"I'll give you that one," she agreed, though she didn't back down. "But I know my limitations and my abilities. I'm not really in that much danger. I'm cautious."

He held her gaze for a long moment as they stood motionless on the sidewalk. He was still frowning, but rather than be annoyed, she thought it was sweet that he was concerned for her safety.

How strange? Any other man questioning her ability to keep herself safe would have pissed her off, but not Andrew. She wasn't sure why, but she had a sneaking suspicion that she couldn't allow to take form right now. She had to see to her people first. Her duty trumped her personal desires this time.

A change of topic was in order. Right away.

"How far to the doctor's office?" she asked.

His face looked pained for a moment longer, then cleared. He gestured behind her with one hand.

"We're here."

CHAPTER EIGHT

Drew wasn't quite ready for the way the other members of Jetty's hunting party looked at him when he ushered her into the doctor's office. They'd been quiet on the breakneck boat ride back to shore, clustered around Sirena mostly, while he and Jetty were in the wheelhouse. Since they'd all left the boat at the dock, he hadn't really thought about them, but now, he realized, they were giving him cautious looks that he couldn't quite interpret.

Instead of dealing with the women, Drew decided to stick with the males in the office—the doctor, Sven Olafsson, who was a polar bear shifter, of all things, and two guys who were assisting him, Peter Zilakov, a big-assed Russian bear, and Gus, the closest thing Grizzly Cove had to a priest. He was the shaman who worked with both the local Native tribe to the south and the residents of Grizzly Cove. His bear was something special—a rare white-ish bear that most called a Spirit Bear. Drew thought he was a little spooky, but in a good way.

Both of the assistants had field medic training, as did a few other members of their community. Drew figured they'd been closest to render aid when the call had come in.

Peter saw him and came out of the treatment area, stripping off his bloody gloves and tossing them in the hazardous waste container. His expression was reassuring, though he frowned.

"She will live," he told Drew, coming right to the point, his words lightly accented. "The injuries are bad, but she's a fighter, this one." Peter almost smiled.

"Can I see her?" Jetty had come up beside him.

"In a few minutes. Your comrade, Beth, is just helping Sven learn the ways of treating your people. Once we got the water salinity right, she began responding very well." Peter did smile that time, at Jetty, and Drew's bear wanted to growl. "They're just cleaning her up, and Gus is doing his magic. Once he'd done, you can all see her."

"Magic?" Jetty frowned up at Drew. He liked that she turned to *him* when she had concerns.

"Gus is our shaman. He can help her," Drew explained.

Just at that moment, Gus stepped out of the curtained area, looking tired.

"Jetty, this is my friend, Gustav. We call him Gus." Drew made the introductions as Gus seemed to regain some of his strength. He must've been working magic to be so drained, but he smiled at Jetty and shook her hand.

"She's out of danger," he said quietly. "I think she's lucky she ran into one of the smaller creatures. Not only were you able to fight it off, but it had less of a magical punch to it, which I was able to counteract. She'll be okay, but if you'll excuse me, I have to sit down now."

Drew reached out to support the shaman, helping him into Sven's private office, where there was a couch, as well as the desk and some chairs. Jetty didn't follow, for which Drew was grateful. He'd seen Gus extend his magical energies before. He knew the shaman would be okay with a little rest.

He helped Gus to the couch, then went over to Sven's mini fridge and got a can of pop and some snacks, leaving them on the low coffee table in front of the couch. He opened the soda can and unwrapped the jerky and individually wrapped mini cheese blocks, leaving them on a plate within easy reach.

"You gonna be okay, buddy?" Drew asked, noting the women moving outside the office, toward the curtained area, which was now open.

"Yeah. Thanks. I'm fine. A little rest, food and sugar…" he reached for the pop and took a long swallow, "…to restore my energy, and I'll be good as new."

"Drew?" He looked up to find Jetty leaning against the door frame. "Sirena wants to talk to you."

With a last questioning look at Gus, Drew straightened.

"Go ahead. I'm okay," Gus replied to the unspoken question.

"Would you mind some company? I think

Beth needs to sit down too. This whole thing shook her up quite a bit," Jetty said, reaching out a hand behind her to draw the woman called Beth forward.

Gus smiled. "I don't mind at all," he replied, turning to address Beth. "There's water and pop in the small fridge over there, as well as some food. Feel free to raid Sven's stash."

Beth gave them all a shy smile and headed for the small fridge near the desk. Drew left with Jetty, glad Gus at least had some company, in case he wasn't quite as *okay* as he claimed.

Drew put his arm around Jetty's waist and went with her toward the cubicle where Sirena lay against the white sheets of an adjustable bed, propped up almost into a sitting position. Her friends clustered around her, but parted when Drew approached. Sven was off to one side, adjusting an I.V. drip. Saline, Drew noted, with a hit of strong antibiotics, which was Sven's way of playing it safe in case some stray microbe dared attack her wounds.

"Ma'am," Drew said politely as he met the older woman's gaze. Sirena wasn't too much older than Jetty, but she definitely had an air of authority about her, even injured and sitting in a hospital bed.

"I wanted to thank you, Andrew, for coming to our aid. I don't want to think what would have happened to us if we'd had to face the bigger creature, if a small one could do this to me." She gestured to her bandaged limbs.

"It doesn't bear thinking about," Drew agreed. "I'm just glad I was in the right place at the right time to give you ladies a hand."

Sirena smiled, and suddenly, there was a sparkle about her that was very appealing. Oh, she wasn't as beautiful as his Jetty, but there was definitely something about Sirena when she smiled. Drew saw the way his buddy Sven perked up. He'd noticed it too.

"I can see why Jetty speaks so highly of you. Even I didn't realize bear shifters had such strength, though I did not doubt your courage. The way you faced that creature…" Her voice trailed off as her gaze seemed to move into the distance, into the past. "I will never forget that as long as I live." Her voice, too, powerful as it was, seemed to drift away for a moment before she refocused on him. "We all owe you a debt."

But Drew held up his hands, palms

outward, smiling to soften his words.

"No, ma'am. You don't owe me. Like I said, I'm just glad I was there to help."

The last thing he wanted was for these people to feel beholden to him. He'd done his duty, as far as he was concerned, and that didn't require repayment.

Drew noticed Sven on the phone in the corner, speaking quietly. If he had to guess, he would say the doctor had just reported Sirena's status to the Alpha. With any luck, John would show up and take the attention off Drew... But Drew didn't want to leave without Jetty.

Would she leave her leader? Or would she choose her people over him now that they were here? Drew was nervous about the answer to that question.

He stood back to watch the women talk quietly, each of them seeming to want to reassure themselves that Sirena was all right. Even Jetty seemed drawn to Sirena's magic, and Drew began to wonder if her name was more than just a name. From the cultured— almost magical—timbre of her voice, he'd bet she was part sea siren.

Though he had never met one before, there were many stories about such beings having magical voices that were so seductive, they could lure men to their deaths in the ocean waves. He wasn't sure if that's what sirens really did. Maybe they only used that kind of power on bad guys? Or maybe they got their kicks killing people? The former, he could respect, somewhat. The latter could be a big problem.

"Sirena, I was coming out to give you my report on the cove and the people I've met here," Jetty surprised him by saying. "I didn't get a chance to tell you the most important bit of news. The Alpha here—his name is John Marshall—sent me with a message. An offer of safe harbor for our people during this crisis. They call the creature a leviathan, and they're already working with Others to find a solution. They've managed to secure the waters here, as we suspected, by way of permanent wards cast by a powerful mage. They'll let us shelter here."

"And what do they ask in return?" Sirena asked, her eyes narrowing.

"Nothing." The deep voice came from over Drew's shoulder.

He'd known the moment Big John had walked in the door, but apparently, he'd taken the ladies by surprise. Scent cues were probably very different underwater, which was something he made a note to ask Jetty about later.

"Sirena," Drew stepped up, making the introductions, "...this is John Marshall, Alpha and mayor of Grizzly Cove."

"Ma'am," John said, moving closer. The other mer ladies made room for him next to Sirena's bedside. "The offer of safe harbor has no strings attached, as I explained to Jetty. I'm sorry she didn't get a chance to tell you before you encountered the creature, but from what Sven tells me, you'll be all right in a few days."

"Thanks to your people," Sirena allowed, nodding toward the doctor and Drew. "And to you, for allowing us to shelter here." Sirena looked around at the small crowd. "Would you mind staying for a bit so I can learn more of your offer?"

John smiled. "Not at all." He motioned to Drew. "Maybe we can scare up some chairs."

Drew was already moving, getting the folding chairs Sven kept around, plus the few office chairs. Within a few minutes, he had seats for all the ladies and John.

What followed was a detailed discussion

of the kind of sanctuary John was offering to the mer in Grizzly Cove. Sirena's questions were more detailed than Jetty's had been, showing the woman had a sharp mind, even if she was severely injured and obviously fatigued. When John suggested postponing their talk, she objected.

"Please, Alpha." Sirena put one hand out toward John. "I want to send two of my hunting party back out—if they're willing— to get your message through to the pod. They will come looking for us if we don't report in on time, and I don't want any more of my people running into that…leviathan…if I can prevent it. So we have to get all the information now, before my friends go back out."

John didn't seem to like it, but he also nodded, indicating his understanding. After a few more minutes of thick discussion, Sirena seemed to relax a bit. He'd answered all her questions in what appeared to be a satisfactory way. A few minutes later, Janice and Marla stepped forward, volunteering for the very dangerous swim back out to the pod.

Jetty had wanted to volunteer, but she

was torn. Never before had she felt so divided about either doing her duty or being with someone. She wanted desperately to stay with Andrew. She wanted… No, she *needed*, to be with him. But she also wanted to help her people and be there for her hunting party.

She'd never felt the friction between doing her duty and doing what she wanted before. Not like this. Her heart told her to stay with Andrew, but her honor demanded that she at least raise her hand to do the dangerous work her hunting party needed to accomplish for the good of the pod.

But Sirena chose two others to do the swim. Part of Jetty felt guilty at the relief coursing through her veins. She'd be able to stay with Andrew, but at what cost to her honor?

"Jetty." Sirena called her name as she doled out assignments, and Jetty feared reprisal for not volunteering to go back out to find the pod and pass along the message. "Since you've made friends here, I think you should continue to act as a liaison. If large numbers of our people decide to shelter here, the town needs to be ready."

"We've already begun discussing

preliminary plans," Jetty was glad to report.

"Good. Continue with that. I'll help, when I can, but I will be the first to admit, that beast took a bite out of me both physically and energetically. I'm running on the infusion of magic from Gus right now, but he warned me I'm probably going to crash hard when it runs out, which should be any time now. When that happens, I'm going to be a bit worse before I start to get better, or so the doctor assures me." Sirena gestured toward the tall blond doctor hovering in one corner, within easy reach. He stepped a little closer.

"I'm going to watch over her," Sven stated boldly. "She'll be fine, but she won't be up to much for the first few days, so set things in motion now, milady, and then, you must rest."

Drew looked sharply at his comrade. "Is this normal?"

"A byproduct of the healing magic Gus had to perform. The creature had spread some taint into her system, but Gus was able to counteract it by infusing her with his magical energy. These few moments of clarity are the result of that healing, but it won't last." Sven looked grave, his sparkling blue eyes concerned.

"So, you see, I'm running on borrowed fumes here." Sirena chuckled, her energy leaving her even as they watched. "I won't be much help until I start to recover. Jetty, you have to represent us to the bears. Set things up. Get them ready for the pod, if they decide to come. You know what to do."

Suddenly, she had a mission. One at which, Jetty knew she could excel. Honor was satisfied. She would be able to fulfill her duty to her people while, at the same time, satisfying her personal desire to be with Andrew. Thank the Goddess.

"I'll do my best," she promised Sirena. "Don't worry. All you need to do now is rest and heal. I'll check in on you as often as I can, and when you're feeling better, I'll have everything prepared. I promise."

Jetty placed her hand on Sirena's arm, in a small space between wads of bandages. Sirena covered Jetty's hand with her other hand, bandages and all, meeting her gaze. Jetty could see the fatigue quickly sweeping over her friend and leader.

"You're a good friend, Jetty. Do us proud."

"I will." As Jetty spoke, Sirena seemed to

slip into slumber.

Jetty looked up at the doctor. He'd moved closer, closely monitoring the electronic readouts that were connected to the many sensors they'd placed on Sirena's body. He nodded to Jetty.

"She's all right. Sleeping naturally. I won't leave her side, ma'am. Not until I'm sure she's completely out of danger," Sven promised, his tone very serious.

"Then, she's still in danger?" Jetty asked, worried.

"I won't lie. There's always a risk with injuries this extensive," Sven told her. "But I'm confident that we got to her in time. Gus did his thing, and the evil taint has been chased from her body. Now, it'll be up to her, but I'm very confident that she'll be fine, given lots of rest and a bit of time."

"I'll stay with her," Beth spoke up. She'd come back into the treatment area and looked a lot better than she had before. "I was a nurse-companion to an elderly lady for a few years when I lived on land. I know how to help someone who's stuck in bed. And I can sit with her when the doctor needs to rest."

Beth was the youngest of their hunting

party, a somewhat shy girl. They were all teaching her the ways of the ocean, since she'd only joined them less than a year ago. She'd spent most of her life on land, and two of her sisters still lived on an island near Seattle.

Jetty realized the hunting party was looking to her now for leadership. Sirena had given everyone a job to do except Beth, but here was the perfect thing. A job that was important and suited to Beth's skills. It would also give Beth a purpose—something she felt was entrusted to her care. Everyone needed to feel needed, and Beth was perhaps needier than most right now.

"Good. If the doctor agrees, I think that's the perfect use of your talents, Beth. I'm sure Sirena would agree." Jetty spoke softly, in deference to the sleeping patient.

They left Sirena in the care of Sven and Beth. Gus was sleeping on Sven's couch when they left, and Peter was watching over him. Everyone who needed looking after was in capable hands for the moment, and it was time to make plans.

With Sirena and Beth at the doc's office, that left Drew with Jetty and the two ladies who were going to make the dangerous swim to report back to the pod. Marla had red hair, and Janice was a blonde. Both were pretty and had athletic builds, and were exceptionally quiet around him, eyeing him with a bit of suspicion, if he wasn't mistaken.

He hoped to alleviate some of their fears, given a chance. He figured a shared meal was a good place to start.

To that end, Drew ushered them all to the bakery, where he told them to order whatever they liked, his treat. Nell Baker packed up their order to go, and Drew escorted the women back to his boat. He had to move it from the town dock back to his own private pier.

He figured the women would eat at his place while they strategized the safest way to get them back out to sea in the vicinity of their pod. He knew they wanted to swim the whole way, but he couldn't, in good conscience, let them do that. Not when he might be able to deliver them closer, with more safety. He just had to convince them it was a good idea.

He figured he had his work cut out for him.

Janice helped him tie up the boat, her

skills indicating that she had prior experience with boats. Both women struck him as very capable and more obviously warrior-like than Jetty, though she was definitely in charge. The other two looked to her for permission to enter his house, and Jetty's small nod wasn't missed by Drew or the two who sought her guidance.

Though his house hadn't been designed for guests, the ladies seemed to like it. Marla was the first to offer a compliment on the decorating, even unbending enough to send him a guarded smile.

By the time they'd shared the impromptu meal, they were all chatting amiably. Marla and Janice seemed to relax as Jetty talked with them about the town. Drew didn't bring up the subject of their proposed journey back into the ocean until they were all sipping fresh coffee and eating the sweet treats Nell had added to their order.

"When do you plan to go back out?" Drew asked, trying for nonchalance.

Marla answered, though she and Janice looked at Jetty first. "Sunset, I think. Or just after, to help prevent any possibility of being spotted."

"All right, but I want to drive you out

there on my boat. As close as you'll let me come to where your people are."

Marla and Janice seemed upset as they looked at Jetty. They didn't speak, but seemed to expect Jetty to object.

"He's right," Jetty said, sighing heavily and running one hand over her hair to push it back from her face.

"But—" Marla objected, but Jetty didn't give her a chance to say much.

"I know." Jetty held up one hand, a gesture asking for patience. "But the whole reason I agreed to let him take me out this morning was because Drew can sense the creature. He can also shield against it and shield others too." Marla and Janice looked at him with suspicion. "That's why we were able to get away this morning. Once you were on the boat, his protection extended to you all."

Now they were eyeing him with something more like intrigue.

"How does that work? Can all the shifters here do it?" Janice asked, a shrewd look in her blue eyes.

"Do all mer have the same strengths and weaknesses?" Drew countered. "As far as I know, I'm the only one with this kind of magical ability. Each of us has our own set of skills. Mine just happen to allow me to steer clear of that creature and hide my magical signature from it, so it won't come looking for me. From everything we've been able to learn, the creature is attracted to magic. That's probably why it's here, since there are so many of us gathered in one place, concentrating the power."

"Makes sense," Marla said, shrugging as she polished off the last of her cheese danish.

"So if we go with you, your protection can shield us until we get in the water?" Janice asked.

"A short distance from the boat, actually," he said. "I can cover a small radius around me. But more importantly, I can sense where the creature is and let you know, when you get off the boat, what direction to avoid, if at all possible."

"I think you should let him take you out as far as the hunting grounds," Jetty added decisively. "Maybe even a little farther." She was looking straight at her two comrades now. "We can't divulge the exact coordinates of the pod's current safe hold, but he already knows where our hunting grounds are from this morning's action."

Damned if she didn't sound like a commando planning a raid. Drew thought it was sexy.

CHAPTER NINE

For the second time that day, Drew drove his boat out past the mouth of the cove and took stock of the magical currents only he could feel. Jetty was at his side, offering advice on where to drop off their two guests, but speaking quietly. Maybe she sensed what he was trying to do. It took a moment of focus to feel where the danger lay.

He blinked and looked at her. She was watching him closely. "Do you know where the creature is?"

"I think so." He motioned toward the ocean chart he had displayed on his left. "The big one is in this area right now. Some of the smaller ones are clustered here." He pointed to another area on the map that was near where Sirena had been attacked earlier that day. "There could be a few outliers, but I won't be able to sense them until we get closer to them, if at all."

"Okay. Then, we need to go here." She reached across him to point to the chart. "This is the southern end of our hunting range, away from the big creature and most of the smaller ones. Once we get there, you'll be able to sense if there are others nearby, right?"

He nodded. "I know you're very secretive about the location of the pod, and I'm not asking to know where they are. I just hope you'll let me get your friends as close as I can before we send them out there into Goddess-knows-what. I don't want to see anyone else hurt today, and that leviathan, and its little friends, are probably still pretty fired up about this morning."

"I trust you, Andrew." Her voice was firm but soft, her gaze speaking of more than just this moment. "But you know I have obligations to hide the location of the pod. I'll get us as close as I can without breaking my vow of secrecy. With your help, Marla and Janice are much safer than they would have been swimming out by themselves, so you've already cut the danger by a big margin."

Drew didn't like that, but he understood. "I just wish I could take the risk away completely, but nobody's figured out how to kill that thing yet." He wanted to cuss, but refrained considering the ladies on board. "Or banish it. The intel Big John's received so far says it can't be killed, only banished."

"Well…" her tone was almost philosophical, "…someone figured it out before, right? I mean, the thing was banished once before, during the last battles with the Destroyer. So we know it's do-able. We just need to find the right weapon or person or team…or whatever…to do it again."

"You make it sound so easy," he quipped, sending her a rueful smile.

"Yeah, I know. But I have confidence the Lady will help us. Evil can't win this time. We have to stop it, in all its forms."

Now he could believe she was a huntress. A warrior. She had that determined stare as she looked out over the waves. She was fierce. And he couldn't love her more.

Jetty directed Andrew and his boat as

close to the area where the pod was currently dwelling as she dared. Marla raised one eyebrow at her in question, but Jetty knew what she was doing. She trusted Andrew with her life—and the lives of her friends. She knew he wouldn't betray them, but she'd sworn a vow to keep the exact location of the pod a secret.

She brought them close, but not directly over the grounds. She only waited for Andrew to do his sensing thing before wishing Marla and Janice a fond farewell.

They were just about to dive in when Andrew came up to the rail.

"I know you'll need time to explain everything to your people and for them to make a decision. I'll come out to these coordinates every day at dusk for the next week and stay until the sun sets. If you run into trouble, you can find me here, shielding. If anyone wants a ride into town, I'll take as many as fit on the deck. Or if they want to swim in, I'll act as escort, spreading my shield as wide as I can to cover as many as I can."

"You're really serious about this, aren't you?" Marla challenged. "We've been out here all along. We haven't had any trouble before today."

Andrew frowned. "Maybe so, but now that the leviathan knows you're here, the trouble may only just be starting for your people. I don't want to see anyone killed by that thing, so I'm offering my services, and my magic, to shield as many as I can on the dangerous trip to the cove. I think the leviathan and its minions will be watching for your folk now. It got a taste of Sirena this morning, and it'll probably be looking for more."

Janice shivered, and even Marla finally seemed to take him seriously. "I'll tell them." Marla nodded at him, and Andrew finally retreated to his wheelhouse.

Jetty took charge of her friends' discarded clothing and stuffed it in a bag while the two mer shifted and swam away. She was worried about them, but didn't see any other way to get the message to the pod. And she greatly feared Andrew was right about the trouble having only just started for the mer in the Pacific Northwest pod.

Andrew turned the boat around and headed back toward shore. They talked quietly as he steered the boat back into the cove, and then to his private dock. He cooked dinner for her on the grill while she set the table. They passed the evening comfortable in each other's company.

Jetty called over to the doctor's office using Andrew's phone, to check on Sirena and let Beth know the others had gotten to the area near the pod okay. Beth would tell Sirena when she woke. For now, Beth wasn't leaving Sirena's side, acting as nurse, companion and watchdog.

Beth would figure it out pretty soon, Jetty thought. The young mer woman would figure out that the bear shifters of Grizzly Cove weren't all that much different than the mer. Oh, the bears were magical, and they had secrets of their own, but they were good people, willing to help others.

It hadn't taken Jetty long to learn that for herself. Of course, she had the added benefit of being around and, now, *with* Andrew.

She'd watched him from afar for a long time, fascinated by his presence on her patch of ocean. She hadn't really realized why she'd been so drawn to him, but the effect hadn't lessened once she spoke to him. In fact, the attraction only grew stronger the more she was with him. And now that she'd been his lover, she knew deep inside that she would never have another.

Wait a minute…

Just like that, the light went on in her mind. She suddenly realized why she hadn't been able to stop spying on him, or why she wanted so much to be in his presence—and in his bed.

He was her mate. Sweet Mother of Oceans.

They made love that night with a new intimacy. Now that they'd learned the basics of what each other liked, they were free to explore and cover new ground. They also didn't have to rush. Jetty didn't have to leave the next morning, and they could even sleep in, if they wished.

They had time now. Time they hadn't really had the first night they'd spent together.

Had that been only yesterday? Had her life changed so much in just a day or two? Had she gone from watching the sexy fisherman from afar to sharing his bed in so short a time?

Jetty had grown up in the human world. Even though she was mer, she'd been raised among human values and standards. She'd never slept with a guy on the first date before, much less started thinking about keeping him forever.

Could she keep him? Would he want to be with her...exclusively? Was his bear thinking *mate*, too?

She had no way of knowing, short of asking a direct question, and she didn't have the guts for that right now. She didn't want to scare off the best thing that had ever happened to her.

Dirk the Jerk was ancient history. Her instincts told her, in no uncertain terms, that Andrew was nothing like Jerkface. Andrew didn't seem to realize how goshdarn sexy he was. She'd never seen him look in a mirror, or any reflective surface they happened to pass, and check himself out the way Jerkoff had done constantly. When Andrew talked to her, he was fully present in the conversation, really listening to what she had to say. He wasn't thinking ahead, a vacant look in his eyes as he planned what he was going to say or do next like his Jerkness.

Being with Andrew had somehow healed the scars on her heart from trusting the wrong man. She hadn't realized it could be that simple. Time away from land and one spectacular man had done what all the sympathy from her friends and family couldn't. She was over the Jerkinator, once and for all. He was ancient history. A speed bump on the superhighway of her life.

Andrew. He was the future. When she looked down that road of her life, she saw him on it with her—a companion to her future. But was she presuming too much?

"I'm glad your people came to the cove." Andrew's voice came to her out of the darkness. They were in his bed, having just made love, lazing together in the moonlight.

"Me too," she replied, content to just be with him. While it was true that she had a lot of questions about the future, this moment with him was too perfect to taint with worry.

"I want you to meet my folks," he said suddenly, catching her by surprise with the enormity of what his words implied. Was he...?

Sweet Mother of Oceans! Maybe he was as serious as she was. No man had ever wanted her to meet his parents before. Even the one she'd moved in with.

"I'd..." She had to swallow to ease the sudden dryness of her mouth. "I'd like that."

"You'll like my mom. She's fierce, like

you," he went on. She turned her head to look at him and could see the strong outline of his profile. He was staring up at the ceiling, tension in the line of his jaw. She wondered what that was about. "She saved me, you know. After I got blown up."

"You what?" Now that had taken her completely by surprise. It seemed this night was one for surprises—not all of them pleasant.

"I stepped on an IED. It exploded and sent me thirty feet into the air. My legs were shredded, the bones so broken the human doctors said it was like putting Humpty Dumpty back together. But they called Mom, and she insisted they not amputate. She fought tooth and claw with them, but she's a force to be reckoned with and they succumbed to her will. Then she discharged me from Walter Reed and flew me home to Wyoming. The military didn't know what hit them when she breezed into town and right back out again with me in a hospital bed, barely conscious."

Her heart went out to him. "I didn't know you'd been hurt that seriously," she said softly, putting one hand on his shoulder.

She was encouraged when he placed his

hand over hers and held it there. She didn't want to say too much, lest he stop sharing. She sensed this was hard for him, and she wanted to ease his burden, not ask a bunch of questions and make it more difficult.

"It was my last mission with the unit. I didn't exactly go out of the military on my own terms." He shrugged and she felt the motion under her palm.

He was so warm and vital. So alive. She couldn't imagine how badly he'd been hurt—and what it must've taken to regain his health, his mobility…his life. He was a survivor. A man to be admired.

"I told you Mom was a priestess. She put everything into healing me. She called in favors from friends and former students. She had all sorts of people coming to see me. To help me. And I was an ungrateful little SOB most of the time. I don't know why she put up with me and my attitude."

He paused in his story, and she squeezed his shoulder in support.

"I can tell you why," she said softly. "It's because she loves you."

How could anyone not love this man? He'd been through so much and still found it in his heart to help others. He hadn't had to risk himself the way he had in safeguarding her hunting party and her people. He'd done it out of the goodness of his heart, his soul. He was something special.

"Yeah." He chuckled low in the darkness. "I guess so. And I love her. And Dad. You'll like him. He's the strong, silent type. Or so Mom claims. Of course, she talks enough for both of them, but he doesn't seem to mind. Dad's a man of few words."

"My parents are a little bit the opposite," she ventured. "I'd like you to meet them too." She bit her lip, unsure how much to say. "I mean, as soon as I call them, they'll probably be up here like a shot to visit with the pod and check on me. They made me promise to call home on a regular basis."

Andrew moved, putting his arm around her shoulders and tugging her closer. She was enveloped in his hug, which made her feel special...and loved.

"You know, if we're talking about meeting each other's families, then I guess we're both pretty serious." His tone gave nothing away, as if he was feeling her out on the topic.

She turned in his arms, propping herself up on her forearms to look at him in the light of the moon coming in through the window. He was so handsome he stole her breath for a moment. But it was the fire in his eyes that made her warm all over. It was time. Time to be open about her feelings and see if... Oh, hell, it was time to take a leap of faith.

"I'm very serious about you, Andrew. My instincts tell me you're someone important. Someone I could easily spend the rest of my life with...if you feel the same."

His arms tightened, and a smile spread across his face.

"Oh, honey, I definitely feel the same. My bear has been beating me over the head with it practically since I first saw you." His voice dipped low. "You're my mate."

The sexy growl from his inner bear that accompanied his uncompromising statement set her senses on fire. Joy sizzled through her veins, and happiness flowed from her heart throughout her body.

"You're my mate, too, Andrew," she admitted, feeling oddly shy. "I...I love you."

He kissed her then, pulling her head down gently and claiming her lips with his. When he let her up for air, he whispered against her lips, the most intimate of declarations.

"I love you too, my pearl."

They kissed for a long time, the languid declarations of love turning into something hot and exciting. Her body was slick with wanting as he joined them together, rocking her slowly, increasing his rhythm with devastating leisure. She came around him three times at least, before she lost count.

The slow, steady presence of him within her made her feel—for the first time in her life—as if she didn't know where she ended and he began. Her lover was part of her in every sense. His body possessed hers, but their souls seemed to be communicating on some deeper level.

He just kept stroking, his confident, steady movements driving her wilder than she'd ever been before. She thought maybe she'd clawed at his back at some point, eliciting that sexy growl that sent her senses into orbit. There was nothing more attractive than knowing she had power over her lover…just like he had power over her.

They were a union of equals. Both submitting. Both dominating. Sharing the burden, and the pleasure. She thought maybe—when she could think at all—that it was a good metaphor for the way their lives would be together.

It was clear that Andrew didn't see her as an appendage. She wasn't arm candy, easily replaceable with a newer, better model. She was to him what he was to her...everything.

And he showed her that, again and again, all through the night.

Occasionally, they slept, wrapped in each other's arms. Comfortable, for the first time in her life, with someone she fully expected to grow old with. She had no doubts. Her beast half and her belief in Andrew washed away all the doubts Dirk had planted. This was her fresh start. The beginning of the rest of her life.

And what a great life it was going to be.

At some point in the long, miraculous night, Andrew turned to her, stroking her skin in the soft moonlight. His eyes sparkled with the love they'd finally expressed in words as well as in deeds.

"I'm going to call my folks soon. Maybe later today. Do you think you're ready to meet them? I don't want to pressure you, but I want us to be official. I want everyone to know we belong to each other."

She could have wept at that moment,

with utter happiness, but held it together. "I'd like that. And I'll call mine too. I'm sure they'll want to celebrate with us. My dad might give you the once-over though. He's very protective," she warned him.

Andrew laughed, and she could feel the joy spreading from his soul to hers. He hugged her close and rubbed circles on her back.

"You know…" His tone had turned contemplative. "My mother might've saved my life and fought for my soul, but you're the one who brought me all the way back." His whispered words touched her heart. "I went out on the water day after day, searching for peace. Looking for something I couldn't find on shore, or within myself. I think…" He paused, seeming to struggle for words. "I think I was looking for you."

CHAPTER TEN

Jetty woke just as dawn kissed the sky. She felt glorious. Her mate was with her, and she wanted to greet the day with all the joy that was inside her. She wanted to do something special for Andrew. He'd been so good to her, doing all the cooking and taking care of her so wonderfully.

Tiptoeing out of the bedroom, she went downstairs and started making coffee. She was about to check the fridge to see what she could throw together for breakfast when she glanced out the back window at the waters of the cove, and stilled.

Was that…?

She opened the back door, walking

barefoot down the path toward the water. Squinting in the pale light of dawn she looked closely at the dock and realized there were at least ten mer in various stages of shift, standing and seated on the dock all around Andrew's boat.

Jetty started to jog toward the dock as she realized her people had come to Grizzly Cove.

Drew picked up the phone and speed dialed the mayor. John was going to have to intervene to make sure no passing humans saw what was going on in the waters of the cove this fine morning.

John patched Brody into the call, and they decided to close off the road into and out of town for the time being. Brody dispatched Zak and Peter to man the roadblocks while he took the task of gathering whatever loose clothing could be found on short notice and brought down to the beach for the emerging mer to wear.

Drew hung up, letting John and Brody work through the logistics of clothing all the water shifters who had no possessions of their own here in town. Finding places for them to stay was something John had asked

Drew to check on, since the main contingent seemed to be gathering on his dock at the moment. Drew would act as spokesman, while the rest of the team got things ready.

Drew walked down to the dock, his hands full of spare clothing. He had emptied his closet and drawers of robes, shirts, and athletic pants and shorts that might possibly fit some of the mer. As a shifter, he knew what it was like to come out of a shift and find oneself with nothing to wear. While nudity wasn't that big a deal among shifters, it also wasn't something they engaged in where humans might possibly see.

And it was too late, he thought, to change the town mission from *artist* colony to *nudist* colony. Although, upon reflection, the latter would've been easier all the way around.

He tried not to chuckle as he approached the dock. Jetty was deep in conversation with an older woman who had not yet shifted, but sat on the edge of the platform, her golden tail swishing lazily in the water.

"I brought some clothes," Drew offered, depositing the pile of fabric, except for one robe, on the end of the dock.

He left it there for anyone who wanted it and strode farther down the wood walkway to Jetty. He could feel all eyes on him as he made his way forward.

Jetty turned and looked up at him from where she was crouching next to the seated woman. Her smile almost made him stumble, but he held it together. Still, that easy, intimate grin warmed his heart. Having a mate was a truly wonderful thing, he realized. It was so much more than he had ever expected. So much deeper and fulfilling.

"Andrew, this is Nansee, the leader of our pod," Jetty introduced him as he approached.

"Ma'am." Drew nodded to the woman, doing his best to be both cautious and polite.

This first contact with the leader of the mer should've been John's job. Drew didn't want to say something wrong and mess up the political side of things.

Jetty stood and took the robe. She turned and held it out for the older woman. Drew tried not to stare as the blonde woman's tail disappeared, along with the luminescent scales that covered her from her face down, disguising her more human…female…attributes. As soon as she had two legs again, she stood and slipped into the robe Jetty held for her, then turned to face Drew.

"Nice to meet you," Nansee said, holding out a hand for him to shake. "I've heard a lot about you from Marla and Janice. Thank you for assisting their hunting party."

"It was my honor, ma'am," he replied quietly.

"Jetty tells me you two have formed an...attachment." Nansee seemed to be testing him, if that sidelong look was anything to go by.

This was it then. Time to fish or cut bait. Drew had never stepped back from a challenge in his life and he wasn't about to start now.

"Yes, ma'am. We're mates." He heard the strength in his voice, and he was well aware that all activity on the dock had come to a sudden standstill. Everybody was listening in. Great.

"You sound so sure," was Nansee's rather vague comment.

"That's because I've never been surer of anything in my life, ma'am. Jetty is my mate, and my bear side knew it almost from the first moment I laid eyes on her. Or don't you mer folk know your mates as quickly as we bears?"

He wasn't afraid to challenge the leader of the mer, just to let her know that he wouldn't be easily intimidated or pushed around. If Nansee thought she'd be able to come in and lord it over the bears of Grizzly Cove, best she learn right here and now that she had another think coming.

She eyed him for a moment longer, then smiled and seemed to relax. Some kind of silent assessment had just happened, and he suspected he'd passed some sort of test, but it was very different than the more blatant dominance challenges among bears. It was going to take some doing to understand the ways of these sea dwellers, but Drew looked forward to a lifetime spent with Jetty figuring it out.

"We often know within days," Nansee answered. "Even I had heard about Jetty's fascination with a certain fishing boat, and her captain. I'm glad to see her instincts led her to you, and that, in turn, has led to a safe harbor for our people. The Mother of Oceans works in mysterious ways."

"Indeed," Drew agreed. Reminded of the greater issue, he remembered what he'd come down here to say. "I spoke to the Alpha and our police chief on the way down here. They're organizing efforts downtown. Clothing, food, shelter and the like. They've even closed down the road leading in and out of town so no humans will see your people rising from the water except those who live here with their mates. There are three human women in town right now."

"Ah, yes. The famous bakery owners," Nansee said, smiling.

"That would be them," Drew agreed. "I believe they're making up sandwiches for everyone as we speak."

"That would be most welcome. I'm afraid we'll have to rely on your charity until we establish our land connections here. Banking, supplies and so forth. But we're not without resources, and we're willing to pay our way, once we get a little better organized."

"Not to worry," Drew said politely. "We know what's out in the sea, and we won't send any being who serves the Light out there. Not now. Not 'til it's safe again. But you should talk to the Alpha. Big John is organizing the logistics, and he has a team of folks working on this."

"All right." Nansee sighed lightly.

She really was a very attractive woman, if

a bit older. There was something very calm about her, and Drew could see why she led the group. She was solid. He found himself liking her.

"I can see you want me to head for the town," Nansee went on. "I just wanted to stop here first and see Jetty. And meet you, of course. I wanted to see for myself if the reports were true." Her eyes twinkled when she looked from him to Jetty and back again. "Congratulations to you both. I expect there will be a party at some point."

"That's a solid bet." Drew laughed as he spoke, relaxing finally. "But I suspect we should get your folks settled a bit more first before we raise a ruckus."

"Don't worry. We've done this sort of thing before," Nansee said with confidence. "Every time we come ashore, we need a little time to gather our resources, but you'll see. We can live on land too. Or beneath the waters of the cove. Whichever." She shrugged and smiled.

Drew wasn't sure what was going to happen, but this woman seemed both capable and reassuring. He got the feeling she wasn't boasting.

Grizzly Cove was about to change again.

What had started as a community of bears was becoming something much bigger than they'd imagined. Whether or not this was a temporary situation, or the town continued to grow was still up in the air. Drew wasn't sure what he wanted...except for one thing.

He put his arm around Jetty's waist and tugged her close. His heart lightened when she came to him willingly in front of her leader and the other mer still gathered on the dock.

As long as he had his mate by his side, he could take whatever came their way and make the best of it. With Jetty in his life, things looked brighter than they had in a very long time.

He turned to her, nuzzling her nose with his, not caring who was watching. She giggled, and her hands went around his shoulders.

"What do you want, Jet? Will you be one of those living underwater?" he teased her.

They hadn't yet talked about where she'd live, but he knew her heart. If she felt the same depth of feeling he did—and he was reasonably sure by now that she did—she would stay with him. And since he couldn't breathe water...

"What do you think?" she teased right back, smiling up at him.

"I think that as long as we're together, nothing else really matters." Oh, he knew they'd both be fighting the good fight against the leviathan and its minions, if necessary, but it all boiled down to that single sentiment. Together, they could face anything.

"Good answer." Nansee's voice came to him as if from afar. He looked to the side to find the older woman watching them with an indulgent expression on her face. She was smiling, which he took as a good sign. "You know, she doesn't have to live underwater with us. Land or sea, a mate's place is with their mate. We won't hold your landlocked state against you, bear. Promise."

At this, all the mer started to laugh, their musical voices filling the shore with a joyful sound, mirroring the joy in his heart. His mer had changed him. She'd brought happiness to a lost soul and healed the broken places within him, when he thought nothing would ever be able to fix him completely.

Nansee would still have to talk to John, of course, but Drew was happy to leave the politics to the leadership. They'd figure things out. Drew would help in whatever way he could, and he knew Jetty's warrior spirit would keep her in the thick of things too. He liked that. They could work together, live together…just *be* together.

"I love you, my pearl," he whispered for her ears alone, right before he swooped in to steal a kiss while the mer cheered…

EPILOGUE

Nansee and her top people held a series of meetings with John and the town council. Drew was part of the council, and Jetty came along with him to the meetings as representative of her hunting party, since Sirena was still laid up at the doc's.

The entire pod had come to the cove, most staying beneath the water, setting up places to live out of the way of casual observers. A few were laying out buoys to mark off safe paths for boat traffic. Drew had worked with Jetty and the mer assigned to the task, since he had a vested interest in knowing where it was safe to steer his boat in the now-densely-inhabited waters of the cove.

When the mer set to work, things started happening fast. Nansee had sent a group to Seattle in a borrowed vehicle, with John's approval. They came back loaded down with bags and bags of clothing and all sorts of business contacts.

Within a day of their return, a small branch office of a big national bank had opened in a disused corner of one of the art galleries, complete with an ATM. Construction plans for a larger permanent bank building were being fast-tracked, and the land had already been set aside. They'd signed a lease for a term of years, renewable subject to the agreement of both parties.

Grizzly Cove was not only getting a shifter-run bank, but another of the mer was making plans to open a small beachfront hotel that could accommodate the occasional paying guest—human or otherwise—as well as any water-dwelling mer who wanted to spend the night on land once in a while. They were including plans for private swim-up access, as well as special rooms on small piers, designed especially for mer sensibilities.

Work had started on a large boathouse-slash-gift shop, which would stock clothing for those who wanted to come out of the water. The back rooms were going to be built on a pier, over the water. Mer could swim up, enter the structure in complete privacy, then shift and dress, coming out ready to walk the streets of town without raising any eyebrows.

Once they set to work, the mer were industrious, and they seemed to have a lot of cash too. Many had tried to hire bear shifters to build their structures, but the guys in town who were able worked for free, or much-reduced rates. Everybody felt bad that the ocean-dwellers been chased away from their home by the leviathan, but they seemed to be getting along well with their changed circumstances for the most part.

The one wrinkle was Sirena. She wasn't responding as quickly as they'd all hoped, and she was becoming a somewhat surly patient. Even Sven had lost some of his legendary patience with her in a very out-of-character screaming match that had been heard by all the neighbors. Of course, a full-grown polar bear shifter roaring in frustration was hard to miss.

After that, some of the more audacious

mer and bear shifters began taking bets on which side would win…fur or fish.

# # #

BIANCA D'ARC

ABOUT THE AUTHOR

Bianca D'Arc has run a laboratory, climbed the corporate ladder in the shark-infested streets of lower Manhattan, studied and taught martial arts, and earned the right to put a whole bunch of letters after her name, but she's always enjoyed writing more than any of her other pursuits. She grew up and still lives on Long Island, where she keeps busy with an extensive garden, several aquariums full of very demanding fish, and writing her favorite genres of paranormal, fantasy and sci-fi romance.

Bianca loves to hear from readers and can be reached via Facebook (BiancaDArcAuthor) or through the various links on her website.

WELCOME TO THE D'ARC SIDE…
WWW.BIANCADARC.COM

Jit'Suku Chronicles ~ Sons of Amber
Angel in the Badlands
Master of Her Heart

Futuristic Erotic Romance

Resonance Mates
Hara's Legacy**
Davin's Quest
Jaci's Experiment
Grady's Awakening
Harry's Sacrifice

* RT Book Reviews Awards Nominee
** EPPIE Award Winner
*** CAPA Award Winner

WWW.BIANCADARC.COM

Made in the USA
Middletown, DE
27 April 2017